THE PIPES

LEVEL UP
BOOK ONE

JJ ANDERS

GRAYTON

This is a work of fiction. Names, characters, places, and incidents are either the product of the author's imagination or are used fictitiously, and any resemblance to actual persons, living or dead, business establishments, events, or locales is entirely coincidental.

Level Up ~ Pipes

DIGITAL ISBN: 978-1-945100-81-9

PHYSICAL HB ISBN: 978-1-945100-85-7

PHYSICAL ISBN: 979-8-338509-34-5

Published by Grayton Press

SUMMARY

Zane is your typical fourteen-year-old; however, what isn't typical is the world he lives in. ECHO is a biosphere where the level you're born into dictates how well you exist. Unfortunately, he was born into one of the lowest levels, the Piper level. Raised by his loving grandmother he struggles to overcome the mysteries of his origins.

The biggest battles of his life begins when he witnesses a murder, thrusting him headlong into a world of danger. As a mysterious donor steps forward to pay for his level education his struggles only increase. Thrown headfirst into learning new skills and intent on moving up the level system, he realizes the higher he goes, the bigger the target he becomes. Not knowing who to trust, he'll have to rely on his upbringing and street instincts, if he's going to survive and make it to the top.

ECHO, a world built from strong metals and elements that have held the many generations of those who had originally volunteered thousands of years before.

These pioneers had been sent out into the blackness of space and set on a desolate planet to live within the biodome of ECHO while vast machines established a habitable world outside. Each volunteer understood that this biosphere would be their world for several generations.

Inside the five circular hubs of ECHO, the world is based on the levels people were born to. Each level provides benefits and hold restrictions. But only wealth is obtained to those who hold higher levels.

Lies and confusion surround ECHO and those who rule it. Deceit swarms around the government while poverty floods the lower levels. For those born in the lowest level they find it has its own benefits, the major benefit is one of ignorance.

To Spencer.

Thanks for staying by my side while my mind pulls me away from this world.

PREFACE

Water drips, air hisses and time passes, yet ECHO remains. Miles of wires acted as the veins for this massive creature. Pipes allowed their creations life blood to flow freely while printers allowed new breath for those hundreds of people trapped inside.

Thousands of years before, the builders had foreseen all the dangers, all the possibilities that might cause destruction to their greatest invention. Each component was perfectly thought out, executed and produced to perfection.

Darkness in the form of mystery swam outside the Biosphere's walls while inside life flourished. Each generation which was born, endured and eventually died in this place, they gave promise to those who would follow.

ECHO

Zane Noman was born on the 97th day in the year 7190. He came into the world screaming as if to protest at the injustice life that fate had already handed him.

Thick black hair covered his small head while his long legs kicked out and his small fists shook. The anger his little voice sounded within the hospital walls was felt by the those who had tried their best to save his mother who had died only seconds prior to his birth. Complications had torn the young mother from the world before the baby's first breath. The medical team had used their advanced skills, but even the machines and strong medicines could not keep the mother alive.

The baby's grandmother, Maria Deller, or Mia to her many friends and extended family, quickly wrapped him in the medical cloth provided, and with tears in her blue eyes, carried him from the birthing room. Behind, she left the body of her only child for the medical team to care for, knowing she would never lay eyes on her daughter's face again.

But the baby needed her, needed her attention. He was her world now. Before Zane, his mother Adalynn had been Mia's all, her pretty daughter had been shy but smart.

Adalynn had been a pipe worker like her father before her, she had labored in the smaller water pipe chambers with the other girls. She had been smart and eager to live life, but now death had been taken her away too soon.

Tests were run on the baby, it was inevitable. While Adalynn had been alive, she had been able to keep the medical teams from performing them, but now... Blood and DNA had been taken from Zane before they had even weighed him. The reason for these tests were simple, over twenty families were trying to unjustly claim the child, but none of that mattered to Mia. Zane was now hers. Her family.

The Medical Register had given Zane his last name only after all the blood tests had been completed. The tests, which confirmed there was no match was relayed to those who had lined up trying to gain from her loss. Noman, or no man's child. Mia knew this was just another slap to the poor child, as if losing his mother wasn't bad enough. Now he would be branded with a name that reminded everyone he would never belong. Zane would never hold a respectable last name, but to be named Noman caused a deep sadness to settle inside her. She had petitioned to the Magistrate to have the boy's last name changed to hers but was denied.

Even bringing the child home from the Medical Hub had been an ordeal. First, she had to verify her own DNA matched with Zane's, then she had to wait for all the other tests to return.

"No male matches" meant that two days after the death of her daughter, she could finally bring her grandson home.

To her dismay, Zane had been welcomed home by an angry mob. Most of the shouting people were families who wished to claim the child as their own along with the daily credits the child would bring them. The hub's Forcers kept the crowd back from her door, but they couldn't stop the angry words shouted at her.

She knew Zane couldn't understand the words thrown at him that day, but her heart died a little knowing these words would be repeated around him his whole life. Words that spoke angrily of things the child was not responsible for. Things that would always keep him separated from others.

Mia knew most of the families were upset because they had failed in trying to claim something that wasn't theirs. The credits this life brought would not line their pockets, fill their bellies, or even bring more comfort to their already large families.

Here, in ECHO in the fifth hub filled with Pipers, a child meant credits. Men earned these by the sweat of their backs, their brains, and their offspring. At least until they were sixteen. Credits dictated where you housed and allowed you more use with the ULTAC processors which provided everyone with food and supplies.

Mia didn't care about the credits or extra food. She had been raised and would remain in her family-owned home which was a two-room hut on the edge of the Pipers Hub. She had lived for forty-eight years in this home, even after her man had died eighteen years ago. What she cared about was that she now had a family back and had someone who needed her once again.

As the years slowly passed, and Zane's sixth year grew to a close, she finally noticed the angry faces had softened towards her. Harsh words were no longer shouted in her or Zane's direction. If speculation and accusations were done, they were now said behind her back. She hoped they were also said away from Zane but worried the sad look in her grandson's clear hazel eyes meant not all words spoken to him were kind.

She knew she spoiled Zane as she raised him. She allowed him to run wild during his early years after his lessons. Children under ten were taught by their families, reading, writing and simple math kept the youngsters home away from the dangers of the pipes because work in the pipes was dangerous. Men worked in the dirty and treacherous lower-level pipes while women and children worked in the steam and water pipes, which were just as dangerous.

Zane loved to run, after she finished his lessons, she would watch him take off to explore his world. She knew he didn't have many friends, and more than once he came home with bruises. Zane refused to speak of what happened each time. Most days he would come back to their small hut with stories of his explorations of the hub they lived in.

He spoke to her of her home as if she had never set foot outside the cozy hut they had. She felt that his young eyes missed nothing, and he would spend hours relaying to her the wonders of their confined world.

"The sphere reaches way up, and I found the tallest

stairs that led behind old man Grayson's house. He didn't even know it was there. He said he thought it led to the main chamber! Can you believe that Mia!" Zane said with wide eyes.

His child's body was already growing tall, his round face soft with youth while his dark thick hair poked out at all angles. She knew she would have to take the clippers to it soon, but she rather liked his hair on the long side.

"The Primer Hub!" He said interrupting her thoughts. Then his face got serious and he turned to study her.

She knew what he saw when he looked at her, her hair had gone mostly gray now; it had once been as black as Zane's. She kept it styled shorter, knowing it kept her round face youthful looking. Small wrinkles lined her eyes, she guessed these were from her long hours behind her sewing machine. Her clothing was stylish, she saw to that as she had made all of it herself. Despite her age, Mia still had plenty of spunk in her and kept fit by selling her sewn clothing all over both the Piper's hub and the Fixer's.

"Mia, have you ever been to the Primer's hub?" His eager eyes would study her as she nodded and returned to repairing one of his socks.

"Yes. Many years ago. I have also been to the Academy hub. Remember, you were born there in the medical facility." She reminded him with a smile.

"Mia, tell me about ECHO." He pleaded; his hands tucked under his chin as he continued to study her.

Sighing, she knew the routine and pretended to ponder his request. This would always prompt Zane to crawl into her lap. When he did, she cast the sock aside as he snuggled into her arms for the story.

"Please." He begged one more time and turn his clear hazel eyes up at her. His little lower lip puckered out in a pout while his arms wrapped around her shoulders.

"Very well, but then it's off to bed." This statement always earned her a smile and a kiss.

"ECHO WAS BUILT by the Colonies hundreds of years ago. These Colonies forged their way into the stars and found homes to terraform."

"That means transfer!" Zane supplied with a smile.

"Yes, ULTAC lab had built ECHO and then looked for volunteers who would colonize this planet they named Amara. Our ancestors were those volunteers." Mia said and rubbed her hand down the boy's back as he drew closer. "Each year we spend inside ECHO is another year the outside world draws closer to becoming our home." She said with a sigh.

Even in her wildest dreams she could not fathom living outside the biosphere. The five hubs that made up ECHO had been all she had ever known of this world.

She had never known the sky which circled above the dome. Never even knew the ground their biosphere rested on, because even the ground below her feet had been made by ULTAC. No dirt, rocks or soil rested under their feet. Instead, there were the hard metals made by the printers, nothing from Amara was allowed inside the domes until the terraforming was completed.

Her people had lived in this biosphere for hundreds of years. Six hundred and fifty-two years according to the records from the first chemically induced transformation. It was unknown how many more would pass before her people would step foot outside ECHO. But life inside continued, and that was all that most concentrated on.

She held her grandson tight as she told him of their home, a home which was able to successfully house over ten thousand in each hub for generations.

Five Hubs make up ECHO. The main hub is where the Primary and most leadership workers live. These top-level people make up the government and all the hub advisors, including doctors and administrators. This hub is the largest and sits directly in the center. In this dome tall buildings stretch high into the vast vault, all covered by green plants and trees which help keep the domes air clear and fresh.

Along the dome's edges sit brightly colored homes where the officials live. New walls and equipment line their dwellings since no expenses are spared in this hub.

The Academy Hub is opposite of our home hub. This hub is used by the medical personnel and professors. All traits not passed down by someone's father can be learned here for the right number of credits.

If you wish to rise above the level you were born into, you must obtain it by attending the Academy. Most, however, only see this hub by ways of visiting the medical facility which means you are ill and in need of treatments. Which again means credits, except child birthing which is free to all.

The Printers are in the next hub. This hub is the most traveled to hub. All used and discarded products can be sent here for recycling. Water and waste are stored here for reuse while the vast printers are maintained and controlled by the administrators.

Printers create everything. They supply repair parts, clothing, equipment, and other daily items. Everything is printed from this hub, but everything costs credits. If you need to replace something, usually you have to pay credits to have it printed. Unless you find a used product, something that had been discarded by someone else.

The Fixers live in the fourth hub. These are clever people who know how to maintain the machines which run the top world of ECHO. The Fixers are employed by all. They repair everything in the city from the air pumps and waste tubes to the carts people use for transportation.

The Fixer's hub is built of discarded equipment from the Primer's Hub. Shiny metal mixed with old which makes up their homes while odd machines line the vast paths that zig and zag around under their dome.

This leaves our hub for last, the Piper hub. It doesn't shine new like the Primer's hub, nor does it hold vast training buildings or massive pools filled with water or waste.

What it does have is buildings and homes that had been repaired by discarded materials. Stairs and walkways twist between the buildings, some trails lead nowhere. Small compact homes line the main walkways on the outside of the sphere while taller apartments rise in the dome's center.

Children run in and out of homes and play games in opened areas. Smells of cooking food procured from the ULTAC Processors drifts out of opened doors. Women found out long ago that cooking large pots of food saved a family their credits. This means stews and soups are the main staples of meals provided.

Men and women who worked down in the lower levels on the Pipes that keep ECHO alive will return home each night, dirty from their days work. The pipes are always dirty.

These men teach their own children, who are ten years of age, the ways of their trade. Mending and maintaining the pipes is a natural trade, one not learned at the Academy, but one handed down generation by generation.

Mia snuggled closer to the sleeping child and knew deep down that the natural trade held by the Pipers was something Zane would never obtain, since he had no father to teach him.

To Zane, the best part of the day was just after dinner and before his grandmother expected him at home to wash for bed. These four hours were paradise to a fourteen-year-old because this time meant freedom. His daily chores had been completed and his deliveries finished.

Zane had grown tall with long skinny arms, which were kept fit because he ran everywhere. His dark thick hair whipped around his face while he jogged here and there completing his chores for Mia.

Mia reminded him daily that he was the image of his dead mother at this age, except his odd eyes. These, it appeared he had inherited from his unknown father. Light tan orbs which often studied the world with wonder and curiosity reminded him constantly of the mystery of his origins.

Zane didn't mind his looks; he found his growing legs helped him run faster and he rather liked his straight nose. Mia often tried to trim his unruly black hair, but he would always distract her whenever she tried to cut his hair with her sewing sheers.

He ran deliveries for Mia each day, taking her customers their ordered clothing or running to the tubes to pick up her special deliveries straight from the printers. Zane loved the days he picked up these orders, it meant running toward the large tunnel that connected his home to the main hub inhabited by the Primes.

After his deliveries were finished, he usually spent a short time with his best friend and distant cousin. Mitch Frankson was twelve, he had been born with weak legs that kept him from working in the pipes. Mitch didn't like to talk about it much, but Zane knew these medical issues made Mitch as much as an outcast as Zane was. This distinction was apparent because they both weren't allowed in the pipes.

Mitch's mother doted on him, even more than her other four children who could train with their father daily down in the pipes. She also understood why both boys wanted to keep their friendship to themselves. She didn't deny them their time together but made sure Mitch's dad didn't find out about the relationship for fear he would ban Mitch from this friendship.

Mitch had one time speculated that it was his constant presence in the house that endured him to his mother. But Mia speculated to Zane once that being needed by someone formed a strong bond.

Zane didn't want to ever tell Mitch, but Mitch's disability was something Zane was thankful for. If Mitch was well, he would go down into the pipes each day like his siblings, then Zane would have been left all alone, all day. And that was something Zane thought might drive him crazy.

What Mitch lacked in strength he made up for with his brain. Mitch was the smartest person Zane knew. Mitch loved to read, he would read anything and everything. Most days Zane would find his friend's blonde head bent over a book or tablet. Sometimes he was reading instruction manuals, other times he was reading government handbooks.

Each day Mitch would have to start home about the time the workers were called out of the pipes. Both boys weren't allowed near the pipes let alone in the vast tunnels which made up the lower half of ECHO.

With no father to teach Zane the trade, and with Mitch's disability, this meant both boys found themselves restricted to the hub. Mitch spent his days reading books and pouring over schematics of ECHO while Zane was left to do odd chores for his grandmother. Zane didn't mind, helping Mia always made her happy. He also didn't mind being alone and used his days inventing cool tools or machines, which always kept him from boredom.

But every day, just after the workers abandoned the pipe tunnels for the comfort of their own homes, Zane would sneak down into the vast caverns. Zane loved the pipes which consisted of vast tunnels that twisted and turned. They had so much room for his young imagination that often he found himself late for bed, but Mia never scolded him.

After four years of exploring, he knew most of the twist and turns of the pipes by heart, not only the pipes under his hub, but the two nearest hubs as well. The Primer's hub was the largest, and he thought the pipes under this main dome the most interesting.

He knew that the tunnels filled with larger pipes kept that dome in working order. Zane had been shocked to see that even under the main hub you could find grime littered the flooring. Though he had never set foot above the pipes in the Primer's hub, he was pleased to say he knew his way around their pipes quite well.

The Printer hub was another story. He had explored these pipes quite a bit but found their pools of water and waste not as exciting as the other hubs. Under the Printer hub you had to know where a pool was, so you didn't end up flooding a tube and drowning.

When he went beyond his own hub, he would travel using his rail rider, a neat invention he came up with two years ago. The rider had a small motor he had repurposed from a broken pump he had found somewhere under the Printer's hub. He had attached the motor to a flat channel and attached a rail hook to the bottom. The rail rider allowed Zane to quickly travel between hubs by way of pod's tracks. Pods were enclosed carts that rode the rails under the vast world.

The pods only ran during the day hours and were shut off at night. When Zane explored the pipes, he always rode the rails using his rider. This allowed him to travel far distances in the short time he was allowed.

To him, it wasn't just the exploration of the pipes, but the discovery of his world that kept him going down into the forbidden underworld of ECHO. Zane also loved all things mechanical. His rail rider was only one of his inventions, he had tons of creations. He built things that helped Mia do her sewing and even a cool tool she used to wash and cut the cloth she used to make clothing for her customers.

Even Mitch used a few of Zane's inventions. Zane had made a crutch for his friend that had a light and a wheel on it. It also had a book holder and kept Mitch's tablet fixed so he wouldn't drop it anymore.

Zane loved inventing as much as he loved exploring. To him, these two activities kept his life filled with adventure and joy.

But joy wasn't always found for him in the Pipe hub.

He knew what the other families said about him. Or more importantly about his mother. Speculation still surrounded his unknown father. He knew several families had tried to claim him when he was born. Some had been related to Mia while others were from the far side of the pipe hub. All these families had only tried to claim him for his credits. But it was their continued bitterness and harshness of their words that still puzzled him.

He had asked Mia once about the anger directed at him. But upon seeing the sadness his question brought to Mia's eyes, caused him to refrain from asking her again.

Mitch had helped shed some light. Mitch explained that many men had wanted to bond with Zane's mom. But her rejection and shyness had been a constant turmoil within the hub.

"I heard she was very pretty, and with your family's hut being set so close to the pod tracks, there were many men eager to claim you." Mitch said with a shrug of his thin shoulders.

Mia had halos around the hut that showed images of Zane's mother Adalynn. The young face did look a little like the one Zane saw in the mirror. But the eyes were dark, not light brown like his. Her smile was nice, and Zane saw the same dimple in the girls left cheek that Mia had.

But he held no memory of Adalynn, only Mia. Mia rocking him to sleep when he was smaller, Mia feeding him, scolding him when he had done something that displeased her. Mia hugging him and caring for him. When he thought of mother, he thought of Mia and Zane was okay with this.

All these thoughts passed in Zane's mind as he grabbed his rail rider and ran to the entrance of the darkened pod tracks. His smile grew as he saw the single light hanging over the conductor's box. Zane saw the box was empty, as usual. Why guard something no one wanted to enter. After all, everyone in the Piper hub had access to the pipes during the day, at night they were too busy living their lives to worry about the dirty and vast abandoned tunnels.

Zane loved to explore the empty pipes where vast tunnels twisted and turned underneath the world he knew. But tonight, Zane was on a mission. Mitch had told Zane about a control switch room for the main hub, one that Zane hadn't seen before. The room was believed to be on the far side of the Primer's hub. To reach the room with enough time to explore and return before Mia grew concerned, Zane would need every second he had.

After walking past the conductor's box Zane neared the platform. Here on the flat metal stand the men and women who worked the pipes each day would wait for the pods which were controlled by conductors.

Jumping off the platform, Zane approached the three rails the pods used. These rails went all over ECHO. Each hub and the connecting tubes had long thin rails lining their underbellies.

After attaching his rail rider to the middle rail, Zane climbed on and using his feet, which now sat on either side of the thin rail, he pushed the switch that started the motor. As his rider jetted off, his smile grew. He loved the way the stale air rushed past him as he flew down the darkened tubes.

Usually he turned on the flash bulb that he had built in the rail rider's front which helped illuminate the tubes.

But tonight, for a while, he let only his chest plate's blue glow outlined the tube for him.

Feeling the kick of adrenaline that came with the speed, he knew that tonight would hold adventure for him.

THE HUB

aking the main tube out of his home hub, Zane felt the excitement of venture take over. It wasn't only adrenaline from the thrill of zipping quickly down the rails, it was also the mixture of being in the forbidden pipes.

This was the one place he was denied access to during waking hours, all because he had no father. No name, no man, no one who would train him in the trade of his home hub. Denied admittance during work hours, Zane got a thrill knowing he knew the dark lower chambers of ECHO's pipes better than most.

He had spent many hours down here, roaming and mapping these vast chasms. He no longer needed the maps he had once drawn and used, because of one time he had gotten so lost it had taken him well into the night to return. Now his mind was the only map he needed.

His keen gift of spatial awareness had saved him when exploring the other tubes too. After learning his own hub's pipes, he quickly realized that all the other hubs had similar lay outs. Pipes and their tunnels all were laid in patterns, a patter Zane had been quick to recognize. Sure, there were small variations, but the main chambers reached out in a familiar grid.

Now, as he raced towards the main hub, he felt free, free from the harsh words thrown his way by his own people. Free from the restrictions of his low level of life. With each minute he felt the negativity fly away from him and the thrill of adventure take over.

His young eyes scanned the way forward as a smile formed on his lips. Yellow blinking lights pointed out the intersections where the rails connected to other routes. After counting twenty, Zane slowed his rider and moved to reach the switch that would transfer his rider to the left rail's pathway.

When he had first used his rail rider, he had had to completely stop and pushed the switch by hand. He had quickly realized that this took too much time and set about creating a handheld tool he called the Stretcher. He called it the Stretcher because it also allowed him to reach all things just out of his reach. This tool allowed him to remain on his rider while reaching the switch and make the transfer.

Smiling now, he gave the long switch a whack with his Stretcher. After hearing the clank of the moving rails, he pressed his foot on the accelerator and once again zoomed down the tunnel.

After another twenty yellow lights, he slowed and prepared to switch rails again. After changing the rails three more times, he finally reached the tunnels he wanted to explore for the night.

According to his clock on his chest plate, only forty

minutes had passed. Knowing he still had lots of ground to cover, he grabbed his rail rider up off the rails and folded it at its center hinge. After attaching it to his backplate's hook he took off down the center tunnel.

Chest plates were one invention he still marveled at. Everyone in ECHO had them, they glowed the color of your hub and held all types of useful tools. Besides the lights, a clock and calendar helped keep your schedule, it also held ropes, hooks and everyday tools like scissors and electrical plugs. The E-plugs used your bodies movement to keep the whole thing charged.

Zane, of course, had modified his chest plate to hold several more things, but he had found that if you added too much, the piece got heavy. That's why he kept his adjustments of his chest plate to a minimum.

Crossing out of the rail tube, he pulled out Mitch's written instructions. Though Zane knew these pipes, Mitch had written down directions to where this hidden control room was thought to be. After memorizing the instructions, Zane put Mitch's map back in his pocket and headed deeper into the dark.

When the blue glow of his chest plat showed the next tunnel, he followed the larger gas pipes to the left. Water pipes which fed fresh water were blue in color. Used water pipes of grey were right below the blue ones, fresh air was green and the air's return ducks were also grey. Electrical was red while heat held a golden color. Zane had learned all these colors from books, unlike most pipers who learned from their fathers.

As he walked Zane felt some of the old resentment at being denied even this knowledge bubble up in him. It had taken him most of the four years of his explorations to learn the fundamentals, but his illegal explorations had quickly taught him more than he thought a regular piper knew.

Taking a right at the next junction, he felt a breeze ahead and slowed his steps. Checking his air gage on his chest plate, he saw the air was clear and quickly moved forward.

When he reached the leak, he saw the joint of the fresh air pipe had wormed loose. Taking his wrench, he stopped his adventure to tighten the joint before finally moving on. Despite his feelings that the pipers treated him unjustly, he still took pride in being a piper.

He knew his hub and its people were the lowest level hub in ECHO. Despite this, he found most piper's he knew took pride in their work. He knew he was an outsider in his hub, but that didn't mean he would let his world die.

After replacing his wrench, he continued for several more yards. Two more rights and an odd left had him finally reaching the chamber he was looking for. The pipe center had all the known pipes snaking in and out of the vast opening. All colored pipes and ducts wound in and around the twenty by twenty room. As he stood there looking at the room, he marveled at its creation. The pipes looked like dancers, each winding and twisting around each other while carrying their precious cargo.

Zane had been in rooms similar to this and quickly found his way beyond the opening and into its center. According to Mitch there should be a subpanel behind the large air duct along the right wall.

He could feel his heartbeat quicken as he drew near. He always got excited while exploring something new.

The air duct was ten feet wide and a foot away from the wall. Only the blue glow of his chest plate gave him light as he turned sideways and started to squeeze into the small space. He ran his hand forward over the smooth metal wall feeling for a door or opening.

"It has to be here!" He hissed as he squeezed in further between the large duct and the metal wall. When his fingers felt a crack in the metal he scooted further inside, so excited he didn't feel the pain of his ribs being squeezed tight.

It was at this time he heard the voices. Panic set in as he realized the voices were close. Too close. If he was discovered here, he would find his nightly visits down to the tunnels at an end. He might even lose his daily credits.

Before he was discovered he quickly shut his chest panel light off and slid further into the crack. Holding his breath, and hoping he wasn't visible, he waited as the voices drew louder.

"You know what this will do!" Came a woman's high-pitched voice. Whoever was approaching didn't fear being discovered down in the pipes after work hours.

A faint golden glow could be seen beyond his hiding place causing even more panic to set in. Golden light was used by people who lived in the Prime hub. If he was discovered by anyone, he could find himself not only void of credits, but in prison as well.

"I know what this means, to all of us." Came a man's deep response.

"I only ask for more time." The woman pleaded.

"How many thousands more do you need?" The man's response held impatience.

"Numbers must be run; we can't just throw this out there. Panic will ensue!"

"You don't get it? You don't grasp what this means." Again, frustration seeped out of the deep voice as Zane scrunched further behind the duct.

"I demand more time!" The female voice sounded hysterical now. "You will not tell him!"

"You don't own me, you may own others, but not me."

"I know your secrets!" The woman threatened.

"I know yours." The man growled in response.

The voices were growing fainter, but Zain could still hear their words bounce off the metal pipes and steel walls.

"You are no longer useful." Came the woman's voice seconds before Zane heard a loud ping. The odd noise was followed by grunting and then the sound of racing footfalls. The steps grew louder indicating that the runner was returning to the pipe hub where he currently hid.

Holding his breath, he watched the golden light grow strong then quickly fade once again. After the light faded back to darkness, he counted to fifty before he was willing to climb out of his hiding place.

All thoughts of the hidden panel room fled his mind as fear of discovery continued to haunt him. Of all the nights he had traveled down in the pipes, this was the first time he had ever encountered someone.

Confident that both speakers had left, he turned his chest plate back on and moved to the tunnel he had enter the room by.

Hoping to make a quick exit he skidded to a stop when he found his retreat blocked by a large body.

. . .

His blue light showed the body was a man's. He was face down on the hard metal flooring with his long legs spread out as blood pooled on the floor below him. When an arm twitched Zane realized the man was still alive and not dead as he had first thought.

Forgetting his wish to remain undiscovered, Zane rushed forward and pushed the man to his back.

When he saw the man blink up at him Zane drew in a quick breath. In the blue light Zane couldn't tell the exact color of the man's eyes, but shock showed in the pale face when he saw Zane.

"You?" The man said and then coughed violently.

The man's dark chest plate had a large hole in its components, which still popped and sizzled occasionally. Seeing the damage now, Zane realized what the loud ping had been, the man had been shot by a blast gun.

"She shot you!" Zane exclaimed as he stared at the blooming blood in the man's chest. Zane had only heard of blast guns; he had never seen one because they were rare and very expensive. Even the Forcers didn't carry these weapons.

"Listen, find Waltson." The man gave another cough and grabbed Zane's hand. "Find him, tell him, tell him I'm sorry." Another cough racked the man's body as he reached up and gently ran a hand over Zane's hair. "I am sorry." He said again and this time Zane thought the man was giving the apology directly to him.

"Hold on, I can go get help." Zane urged as the man gripped him hard.

"No, she controls them. Find Waltson." He repeated as he lowered his head to the hard floor. "You look like her." With this, the man closed his eyes and took his last breath.

"No, I can get help!" Zane urged again and tried to stand but found his sleeve was still clutched in the man's iron grip. "No!"

Now panicked, Zane tried to pull out of the dead man's grasp. As he heard something rip, fear overwhelmed him, and he started to tug and pull harder. When he was finally successful of pulling his sleeve out of the man's grip, he heard another loud rip before he turned and quickly fled.

Zane ran, he ran down the tunnels as if he was being chased. As he raced back to the rails, it was as if his feet knew the way even while his mind kept replaying the man's death.

He was six rail changes away before he finally stopped to calm himself. Dropping down to sit on the hard metal rails, his shoulders slumped as his body started to shake.

Dead! The man was dead! The woman had killed the man!

He had never seen death before, never been near anyone that he remembered who had died. Mia had told him his mother had died seconds before he had been born, but he didn't remember these events. Even when someone died in the pipes, which happened often, he was never there when the body was removed from the tunnels and taken to the medical hub.

Closing his eyes, he once again saw the man's pale face. The man's eyes had looked at Zane with such shock, no doubt from the pain and realization of his pending death.

Zane didn't know what to do now.

If he returned to his hub and reported the murder, then he would be discovered. His nightly exploits to the forbidden pipes would stop. Maybe he would even be accused of killing the man? Maybe they would find some way to pin the death on him? What would happen to him then?

Prison?

He had heard that the prison cells were only for the most dangerous of people, would they put him there? He was only fourteen!

And if they put him there, what would happen to Mia? It was these thoughts of his grandmother suffering because of his imprisonment which caused him to calm down and think.

After taking a large breath, clarity finally reached his youthful and panicked mind.

Nothing could prove that he had been down in the pipes when the man had been murdered. Nothing and no one could confirm he had been down in that room. He had left nothing behind.

He needed to calm down and pretend none of this had ever happened. If he did this, his life, and Mia's would continue like normal.

Yes, the man was dead, but he didn't *know* that man. He didn't know who the woman was that had killed the man. He didn't recognize her voice and hadn't even seen her. He had seen her chest plate light as gold, but there were thousands of people who lived in the Primer's hub.

Surely, he wasn't responsible for reporting the death when so much was at stake for him and Mia. His mind ran through his short life and after taking another deep breath, he wiped the tears from his face and climbed back onto the rail rider.

He hadn't done anything wrong, and he needed to

keep reminding himself of this. He wasn't the guilty one, so no one could ever find out what he had witnessed. No one.

By the time he returned to the Piper hub he had calmed down considerably. If his hands shook as he packed up his rail rider, no one was there to see them. He made sure to wipe his face clean incase his tears had left tracks down his face.

He felt his confidence build as he moved out of the pipes and out into the streets and walkways of his hub.

It took him several more moments before he calmed down completely and build up his nerve to walk into the hut that Mia and he called home. He worried that she would see he had been crying, Mia saw everything when it came to him.

She was bent over her stitching, despite the late hour. Her silver hair glowed in the single bulb's glow and the glasses perched on the end of her nose reflected its light when she glanced up at him.

"About time, I was going to send out the Forcers if you hadn't returned soon." Mia teased then her eyes landed on Zane and she quickly stood. "What has happened?"

Shrugging his shoulders Zane turned and walked over to the small table, grabbing a piece of printed fruit, he popped it in his mouth while he tried to remember what he had planned to tell Mia.

Slowly chewing and then swallowing, he gave Mia a smile. "Nothing. I had a scare with the rail rider. Its charge died and I had to walk to a station before I could return home." With his fingers crossed behind his back, he hoped Mia would fall for his plausible lie. But when she continued to stand there looking at him, he knew his lie hadn't been believed.

"Tell me." She insisted as she walked to him and pushed him down into the nearest chair. Her stern look gave him pause and he knew his prior resolve to tell no one what had happened was only a wish he had told himself.

After taking a deep breath, he felt his body start to shake again as emotions overtook him. When he was finally able to talk, the whole long story came flowing out. He wasn't sure he even paused for breath while he relayed the details to her. His head spun as the details continued to spew from his mouth. Mia remained quiet the entire time until he was finished.

With his eyes closed and his shoulders shaking from misery, he felt Mia wrap her arms around him. Mia was his family, and he knew she wouldn't turn him in to the Forcers. But would she understand why he had left the man's body there and why he had fled the pipes? His head hurt and there was a sour feeling in the pit of his stomach as he waited for his grandmother to say something.

"Zane, my sweet child." Mia murmured as she squeezed him closer to her. "My dear child. I am so sorry you witnessed this atrocity." She continued to murmur words to him while he cried, words that gave him comfort as she held him.

When his eyes finally dried and his shoulders stopped shaking, Mia stood to make him a snack. As she set the biscuits and drink before him, he glanced up and saw her sober face, her eyes were also wet as she returned his gaze.

"Your exploits into the Pipes are done." She sat across

from him at their small table and the expression on her face dared him to argue with her. "No more. I doubt that after tonight you'll even want to go back into the tunnels. It maybe that you can't, when the body is discovered."

"What do you mean?" Zane asked. At the moment he didn't feel like ever going back into the pipes. He sat there and tried to focus on her last statement instead of the dead man's face. "Why wouldn't I be able to?"

"Who knows?" Mia asked instead of answering his question. "Who else knows you journey down there each night?"

Shrugging his shoulders, Zane thought for a minute. Most people who lived within the Piper's hub had no use for an orphaned boy with no father. Sure, several of Mia's family and friends were kind to him, but Zane was a young boy with no real companions, except one.

"Mitch, he knows." He finally answered.

THE LOTTERY

M ia and Zane had a plan. It wasn't much, but between the two of them the idea seemed solid. Zane was confident Mitch was his true friend, he just hoped the boy agreed to the plan and didn't ask too many questions.

Zane spent the morning working his normal chores. Mia wanted to give the appearance to their neighbors that nothing had happened last night. She feared that when the body was discovered, it would also be discovered that Zane usually wandered in the pipes, especially last night. If this was discovered, Zane might be accused of this death. Even the hint that he knew anything about it might cause their way of life in jeopardy.

So, Mia worked her job and Zane ran deliveries. Most hubs used the printers for clothing, but that costs credits, a cheaper way to gain clothing was to have a person make them. This prompted the need for sewers.

Mia, and her mother before her, were skilled in patching and sewing cloth together to make pants, shirts and much more. Most of her clients brought discarded cloth or clothing to Mia and asked for patchwork outfits for their children who had outgrown their prior clothing.

Mia would often buy the discarded clothing from them and use them for pieces she could sell to others who had smaller children. But her big earning was when she traveled with her wares to the other hubs. She only did this once every forty days as the E-shuttle was a high cost which ate into her earnings.

To Zane, the morning seemed to take forever. Each time someone came into the home, where Mia did her business, he feared it was the Forcers coming to take him away. Three of the morning customers brought their children with them for fittings, while a fourth only came to drop off discards for some credits.

"Don't look so nervous." Mia scolded him between customers. "Go, run these over to Sarel's home." Mia handed him a wrapped bundle and scooted him out the door. "And relax." She hissed as he squared his shoulders and took off at a jog.

Sarel lived two walks down and six over from their small home. She had six children and two who were still too small for training in the pipes. Knowing his arrival at the home would come with questions from the children about why he wasn't in the pipes, he lowered his head as he walked.

It was hard for him to see these young eyes full of speculation. Most children bluntly asked him why he was delivering clothes instead of working in the pipes. Those questions weren't too hard for him because most of the mothers would quickly shush their kids and then apologize, embarrassed by their child's bluntness. Usually this type of interaction meant a quick transaction and fast retreat for him.

But the gazes, the speculation in the eyes were everywhere. From most of the women in his hub, he received sympathy, their eyes would go soft and they would call him dear or sweety, as if that would make up for him not having parents. From the men, he still received out right hostility. Some extended family members, most of Mia's or other obscure distant relatives he was treated with what he knew to be a forced kindness.

Now, with a feeling of dreed at the coming delivery, he continued walking with his head down, his eyes on his shoes and the path he walked. When he was three walkways away from Sarel's home, the sound of the APA system sounded, distracting him from his dark thoughts. When the Primary's advisor's face flashed on the hub's screen Zane stopped to study the screen. Each hub had four halo screens along the dome's top portions. These screens were used for the Primary to communicate with the people of each hub. Usually public announcements or emergencies were relayed by the APA system.

The Primary was the title of the person who ran ECHO's government. The current Primary was a woman called Louise Kasher; she was a fifth-generation leader. Her mother, grandfather, great grandmother and great-great grandfather had sat in the seat before her. Before her family had obtained this high level, it wasn't recorded who had been the Primary, but most in the Piper hub didn't care about history.

Luminaries and advisors worked for the Primary, along with each hub's administrators and their assistants. These people in the high levels ran the government along with the facilities such as the banks, employment distributions and printers, along with facilitate the formal education, which was provided at the Academy. All these high-level people controlled the functions seen outside the mundane physical work done by the people who made up the lower levels.

Communication from the Primary's office was rare, usually saved only for special holidays. So, when Davis Elliotson, the Primary's advisor's face glowed high above Zane's head, sweat formed on Zane's back and his pulse quickened.

"Attention." Davis said, his youthful face stern as he looked into the camera. He was a young dark-haired man with dark brown eyes that squinted as he frowned down from the screen. "Attention. Forcers are seeking information regarding a crime taken place last night in the pipes. If anyone has information regarding any activities that happened between nineteen hundred and twenty-three hundred last night, it is recommended you communicate with your hub's advisor." Here the man's brow furrowed, his dark eyebrows almost drew together as he paused. "Until the person who completed this crime is caught, all afterhours access to the pipes will be denied to all." With this, Davis's face flashed once, and the halo screen went invisible again.

Forgetting his current delivery, Zane turned on his heels and rushed back down pathway the way he had just come. Before he had time to think, he was raced down the narrow paths and upon reaching Mitch's home, knocked quickly on the door. Melony Johner, Mitch's mom, who was one of Mia's great nieces, answered with a confused expression.

"Um, I came to fix Mitch's crutch." Zane stated quickly, hoping she believed his lie as he rushed past her and into the back room where Mitch usually sat for his studies.

He breathed a sigh of relief when he found his friend bent over a thick volume book. The book's yellow delicate pages illuminated for his friend to read while a tablet sat next to it for Mitch's notes.

"Mitch!" Zane exclaimed a bit too loud as he crashed into the room. "Mitch." He repeated, this time a bit quieter as he neared his startled friend.

"Zane? What are you doing here?" Mitch asked as his blue eyes turned from the pages to Mitch.

Quickly kneeling, Zane placed a hand on his friends discarded crutch and bent close to his friend's ear.

"Mitch, have you told anyone about my nightly trips?" He whispered as he fiddled with the latches on the crutch, just in case Melony came into the room.

"What?" Mitch asked, confusion covered his face as he watched Zane tinkering with his crutch. "Oh, no. Why would I?"

"It's important. Have you told anyone?" Zane urged as he studied his friend. "Anyone!" He hissed the last word which caused Mitch's eyes to narrow.

"No!" He hissed back. "Why, what has happened?"

Shaking his head, Zane leaned back for a minute and thought. "Nothing. It's just that with this announcement, Mia has forbidden me to travel there again. She wants to make sure..." He stopped and thought for another second. "Never mind."

"Zane. What is going on?" Mitch asked this time he

reached out with his thin hand and grabbed Zane's forearm; his blue eyes wide with concern.

"I'll tell you later, just... Don't tell anyone about my travels." Zane whispered with a shake of his head. "Swear it."

When Mitch quickly patted his own heart, Zane knew his secret was safe with his friend. "What about your mom?" Zane asked and felt the blood drain from his face again.

"I'll ask her not to tell anyone, she will do anything for me." Mitch replied as his eyes turned to look at the small door leading out of the bedroom, he shared with his two brothers and three sisters.

Zane thought quickly of Mia, of how she was willing to do anything for him, he thought of their closeness and realized Mitch and his mom must share the same type of bond. After a moment he nodded once and smiled. Then he quickly leaped up from the floor and dusted off the knees of his pants. "See ya after your studies." Zane said with another smile and ran out to finish his deliveries.

TWO DAYS HAD PASSED before rumors drifted to the Pipers hub that a body had been found in the pipes. Rumors told of an important person or persons who may have been found dead in the vast tunnels. Some even speculated that it had been a robbery where the thief had taken off with thousands of credits. Some of the stories even told of a dreadful plot to undermine ECHO's government while other tales hinted that a deadly murderer was loose in the dark pipes. Despite all the stories, it was unclear what had happened and who, if anyone, was dead.

There was speculation that a piper had died during working hours, something that unfortunately happened way too often. There was also a rumor that a person from the Primer hub had fallen down a tube and died. Most believed this last rumor as it had finally been confirmed after the third day, that the crime had taken place underneath the central hub.

Forcer's yellow tape had blocked the pipe room in question. The workers who were assigned that area quickly confirmed that they had seen the tape and the blood stains on the floor which gave them lots to talk. After they returned home that night, they told everyone who would listen about what they had seen. Soon, speculation quickly flew around the Piper hub.

"Some say he was a high-level counselor!" One woman told her neighbor loudly as Zane rushed past them. His steps faltered at this speculation, but he didn't look back as he neared his own home.

Guilt still ate at him for leaving the man after he had died. Guilt and fear at having been there to witness the death, at hearing the man's last words and not knowing who had killed him. He even feared that the man hadn't been dead after all, that maybe he could have helped save him.

True to Zane's word to Mia, he had not gone back down into the pipes. He had stayed close to home and in his own hub since that dark night. He had discovered that it was easy to stay away from the black gapping entrance to the tunnels. Each time he neared the pipe's entrance, he would break out in sweat and his heart would race until he was several blocks away from the tunnels.

Each day, worry ate away inside him at being discovered. Every time he saw a Forcer, he would grow nervous. When the large peacekeepers would pass him without even casting him a glance, he would quickly breath a sigh of relief.

Each day his nerves grew, it seemed that Mia became calmer. She told him that nothing would lead the Forcer's to their door. Usually her words would calm him, that is until the next time he saw another Forcer.

The more days that passed helped Zane with his worries of discovery, but each night he shut his eyes the man's face would flash before his closed eyes. He started leaving a small light on each night hoping that the light would keep the image away, but it always failed.

Zane felt that the following days crawled slowly by, he attributed this to the long evening hours, hours he had usually filled with his adventuresome travels. He spent most of these hours inventing and playing with Mitch, which helped some. They talked of the hubs, about the equipment's that kept their vast world alive. They even talked about Zane's inventions.

Mitch had great ideas about new computer programs and tools they could build. He helped Zane invent a new program that could help Mia keep track of the clothing she sold. The programed would track a customer's child growth and estimated when they would need to order new clothes.

Mitch helped Zane download the program into Mia's tablet; they only crashed her system once before they got the schedule to accept in the sub program. Zane had burned his left hand a little when the tablets security had sent a small zap along its screen, but the system worked, so far.

Mitch still had studies in the morning with his mother, while Zane had his chores for Mia. This meant that the boys only had the afternoons to play. His time with Mitch did seem to help the passing of time, it also helped him forget the horrors he had seen down in the tunnels.

Six days after the Prime's advisors' announcement had flashed over the APA system, another message came. This one was delivered by Forcer Sargent Master Peterson. Forcer Peterson was a serious military man with short-buzzed silver hair. His stern face flashed on the screen as he addressed all the hubs at once.

"Attention, a reward has been set for information regarding the deadly attack that took place six days ago down in the main hub's pipes on level two. Reward will be given for valid information only, please speak with your hub's advisor if you have any information." With this, the grim face disappeared.

Soon speculation and rumors buzzed around the pipes as dread filled Zane. During their lunch, Mia tried to convince Zane that they still had nothing to worry about.

"Even if your name is mentioned, there is nothing to prove you were ever there." She said, but Zane thought he heard a hint of fear in her voice.

That evening as Zane walked to Mitch's house he wondered, not for the first time, about the man he had seen die. Witnessing a man die had been surreal, but the man's words had all sorts of questions arising in Zane's young mind. His interaction with the dead man, short as it had been, had caused Zane to wonder about his own future. A future, that at this point, he felt held only limitations.

He was a child without a trade, a boy rejected by

everyone who could teach him his hub's business. He wasn't even allowed in the pipes during working hours. This left a big hole in Zane's future, how was he supposed to grow up and have a job, or make a living?

How would he earn credits after he reached the age limit? Would he continue to run errands for Mia his whole life? What would he do after she was gone? How would he ever earn his own credits?

He was so deep in his thoughts he hadn't seen Mitch rushing down the path towards him, as fast as his crutch and bad leg allowed. It wasn't until Mitch was feet from him shouting that he glanced up.

"I got in!" Mitch hissed as his crutch slammed against the metal flooring in front of Zane. "Can you believe it! My mother just got the news! I got in, and I'm one of the youngest to get in so far!"

Confused Zane looked up to see Mitch's blue eyes filled with excitement. "What are you shouting about?" He asked as he saw Mitch do a little wobble before him. "Are you dancing or falling?" Zane asked as he reached out to help steady his friend.

"It's called dancing! I got into the Academy!" Mitch shouted as his skinny legs wobbled again. Zane grabbed Mitch's arm and helped steady him as confusion filled him.

"The Academy?" He asked as Mitch tried to continue his little dance.

"The Lottery, I got picked for the scholarship into the Academy! Free! I will get to go and live there for one year." Here his friend finally stopped and looked at him. "Each year, if I advance to the next level, the scholarship will be extended. As long as I advance each year, it won't cost my parents anything."

"You'll go live there?" Zane asked as Mitch's words sunk in. All of a sudden, his whole world seemed to grow even more constricted. Thoughts of spending his days without his friend seemed to loom ahead of him. These thoughts didn't seem pleasant, at all. Zane envisioned long days without Mitch as the boy continued to talk about the school which was located in the University hub.

"I get a room and food, and my parents get to keep collecting my credits while I'm there too!" Mitch again stopped his little odd dance and frowned up at Zane. "Dad seemed more excited about that, but when Mom told him he would have a son who could eventually be several levels above a Piper, he cheered up."

"But you will come home, eventually?" Zane asked, to him, his voice sounded hallow. He studied Mitch's young face and suddenly felt like a bad friend for only thinking of how Mitch's news affected him. If he were a good friend, he should be happy for Mitch, despite how it could affect Zane. "You will come and visit, right?"

"Of course. There are the allowed holidays, and the two months each year where the academy shuts down for repro-cessing." Mitch answered with excitement. "And we can E-write! All the time." Here Mitch's face finally fell. "Of course, I won't get to see you every day, and you won't have anyone else to play with." Again, Mitch frowned up at Zane who was at least a foot taller than him. "What will you do each day?"

Waving one of his hands, Zane shook his head. "Don't worry about me, I'll keep busy."

"But you don't," here Mitch lowered his voice so only

Zane could hear him, "you don't even get to go into the pipes anymore. What will you do once I leave?"

"When do you leave?" Zane asked and tried not to think about his friend's pending departure. Part of him hoped it was several days from now, which might give him time to adjust to the thought of Mitch being gone. But when Mitch replied that he would leave for school in three days, Zane's heart sunk to the bottom of his stomach.

"Three days?" Zane asked with dreed.

"They say the courses started last week, but some paperwork caused the delay in letting me know about the lottery."

"I'm sure you will catch up quickly." Zane stated with confidence as he saw doubt creep into his friend's eyes.

"But I'm a lot younger than others." Mitch said with fear in his voice. "What if I fail?"

"Are you kidding?" Zane said with shock in his voice, "You're the smartest person I know, chances are you will jump up a level long before the year is up!"

THREE DAYS PASSED TOO QUICKLY, then Mitch was off to the Academy. Mitch's family had thrown a small party for him the night before his departure, Zane and Mia along with several other families had attended.

Everyone brought Mitch gifts, items they thought would be useful when he attended classes. Items such as new shoes and a book bag were the most expensive, while other families provided pencils and paper books. Since no one in the Pipers hub had ever attended the Academy, no one really knew what to get the young boy.

Zane had given his friend a newly built two-way talker, or TWT as he had called it. He wasn't sure the signals would reach across the great distance, but Mitch promised he would try the TWT the first night.

"If it doesn't work, we can try and boost the signal." Mitch promised before his party had ended.

Mitch would reach the Academy hub via a Tram; these machines were used in the connecting tunnels above the levels where the pipes were. The Trams usually transported equipment and supplies but sometimes people used them to travel to other hubs.

Mitch's mother would travel with him; she would help him get settled in the dorms then return that same day. Because of his disability, Mitch would live in one of the dorm rooms right in the middle of campus. Most students lived in dorm rooms in buildings selected based on their hub. With Mitch's disability and the Lottery, it appeared his friend would be given a nice, private room.

The day Mitch went to the Academy, Zane fought with his emotions. Envy was something he had felt his whole life. Yet now he found it was joined with the overwhelming feeling of loneliness.

That night Zane tried his two-way talker and got nothing but static. Discouraged by this, he continued to try it each night, hoping for a signal. He tried using the TWT while sitting on the roof, right outside the joining tunnel, and even near the hub's wall. Still nothing could be heard out of the small speaker to his discouragement. He then tried to boost the signal by attaching discarded metal pipes to the wires, but still nothing worked.

Discouraged buy the TWT's weak signal, Zane passed the days in misery. Mia tried to help his poor mood by keeping him busy, but even as he ran errands around the hub, he brooded about his missing friend.

Five days after Mitch had left, while on an errand of Mia's, walking with his head down because of his sour mood he bump squarely into a stranger. Strangers weren't unheard of in his own hub, after all there were last reported to be over eleven thousand Pipers.

The man quickly grabbed Zane's arms to prevent him from falling to the hard floor. He was old, about Mia's age, but his clothing was odd for a Piper. His chest plate glowed blue, but Zane still thought the man's pants and shirt unusual.

Thick white hair stuck up from the man's head at odd angles, the hair also stuck out on his face in the form of a short beard. Kind, tan eyes looked at Zane as he released Zane's arm.

"Tell me," the man said in a friendly voice, "where is a young lad like you off to in such a hurry and sour mood?"

"Just deliveries." Zane replied as he took a small step back.

"Deliveries? Why aren't you working in the tunnels?" The man asked, the smiling face turned questioning as he tilted his head and continued to study Zane.

This was a question Zane was used to, and one he feared each time. Usually it was asked when he met someone new, someone who didn't know of Zane's unusual circumstances.

Sometimes he would make up odd stories, answers that told of secret missions or special messages that urgently needed to be delivered to the hub's administrator. Stories of adventure and trials which always placed him in the line of a hero. He knew Mia didn't like him to make up these stories. One of these farfetched tales was on the tip of his tongue, but today, he was just too depressed to come up with a wild retort. Instead he just shrugged his shoulders and gave a big sigh.

"Tell me, are you Maria Deller's grandson?" The man asked, his odd tan eyes narrowed as he continued to study Zane.

Zane had to blink once upon hearing Mia's real name, then he nodded and looked down at his shoes. Bracing himself for the onset of sympathy he knew must be coming, squared his shoulders as he looked at the man's shoes. They were clean and made of a material Zane had never seen before. The black was shiny and there were two buckles made of silver that kept them clasp near the top.

"Ah, you must be Zane. Hmm." The man said and grasp Zane's hand in a friendly shake. His pale tan eyes continued to study Zane as he tilted his head again, this time scratching his cheek while he pondered Zane.

Zane knew most of Mia's friends and customers. Then there were the people in their extensive family which amounted to well over two hundred. Giving the stranger another deeper study, he had the odd feeling he knew this man, but when no name came to his mind, he remained silent as he squinted and stared back.

"Who are you?" Zane finally asked, breaking the odd silence. The stranger must have found his question funny because he let out a small laugh.

"My boy, that is a good question." The stranger said. Yet he hadn't provided Zane with the answer, instead he continued to study Zane.

"Tell me, why do you look so sad?"

The question caught Zane off guard, most of the adults who knew him, or his situation, would have tried to brush past with a quick excuse. Some would have asked about Mia and awkwardly listen to Zane's answer then immediately make an excuse. Here was this man, looking genuinely interested in Zane and his answer.

"If you know Mia, then you know why I'm sad." Zane's challenging question caused another laugh from the man.

"Smart boy. My name is Adam. I haven't seen Maria for several years. Which means I am not current in the news here in the Pipes." Adam said with another smile.

Zane didn't recognize the man's name, but Mia did know many people, some from other hubs. Yet he wore the blue chest plate of a piper, maybe he just worked outside the hub? This excuse seemed plausible and Zane finally answered with a quick shrug of his thin shoulders. "My best friend went away to the Academy."

"Ah." Adam said with a quick shake of his head. "Lonely, are you?"

Nodding, Zane watched as Adam bent closer This time, instead of studying Zane's face, Adam looked closely at Zane's chest plate.

"Tell me, what have you done here with your chest plate?" He asked as one of his thin fingers pointed at the additions Zane had made.

"I improved it." Zane said defensively. To his knowledge there was no law against the adjustments he had made.

"Yes, I see that. What does this button do?" Adam asked with interest.

Soon Zane found himself describing all of his

enhancements to the man. He explained the functions and then would show Adam each invention's ability.

Adam seemed genuinely interested in each function of Zane's improvements to the chest plate. He asked questions and wanted to see all of the enchantment's operations. Adam would pause after each demonstration, as if weighing the tool's functions thoroughly before moving on to the next tool.

"I see, you have made some marvelous improvements to this, tell me, what else have you invented." Adam's question prompted Zane to tell him of his other inventions.

He was just launching into a description of his rail rider when he remembered with dreed that he wasn't supposed to tell anyone that he had ever been down in the pipes. Worried his secret would be discovered, he quickly cleared his throat and made an excuse.

"Sorry, Mia will be waiting for me, I'm already late." Zane said quickly and darted a few feet away before he turned and looked once more at Adam. "It was very nice to meet you." Zane said politely.

"I too enjoyed meeting you Zane." Adams said with a quick smile on his face.

Giving Adam one final wave, Zane darted down the path to finish his deliveries, unaware that his dark mood had lifted for a while as he talked to Adam. For the rest of that day, Zane's mood lightened.

SCHOOL

"Zane!" The sound of his grandmother's voice dove down into his dream.

Zane had been dreaming of an odd electrical world, one where the people who walked before him were computerized. Wires replaced blood and chips replaced brains in the people of his dream.

Mitch wasn't a boy, but a computer that kept spitting out vast equations. A long scroll of paper spilled out of the machine Mitch's open mouth as if it held an unlimited amount of parchment.

Even Mia, her short bob of hair had been replaced by a robot version of his grandmother. She sat there sewing not clothing but chip boards instead. When she got finished with an item of clothing, it wouldn't be pants or a shirt, but a whole new functioning robot.

Soon their little home was filled with tiny robots that wheeled around and chirped facts at him. Zane tried to let them out the front door, but Mia kept knitting them into existence faster than he could catch them and shove them out the door.

Just when he felt his dream turn bad, panic filled him as his vision turned dark. Once again saw the pale face of the dying man deep down in the pipes.

"You left me down here!" The man moaned as his dead eyes stared at Zane.

"No." Zane tried to shout but found he couldn't form the word. Instead a stream of paper with computer facts spilled out of his mouth.

"You left me just like your mother left you." The man said and his face was quickly replaced by the image of his mother's pretty face. Pale in death, she stared at Zane as he tried to cry out.

"Zane!" Mia's voice rang out again.

Zane quickly awoke as Mia shook him hard. "Didn't you hear me?" Mia asked as she looked down at him.

Blinking in confusion, he tried to bring Mia's concerned face into focus as he lay on his bunk. For a brief second, he saw a robot Mia instead of the real one. But when he blinked again, he saw his grandmother leaning over him as she turned on the light between their beds.

"Zane! Are you well?' She asked with concern.

"I'm fine." He lied and blinked a few more times, then quickly rubbed his hands over his face as he sat up. "Did I sleep through the alarm?"

"No, we have guests." Mia said as she rose and handed Zane his clothes. "Quickly, get dressed."

After dropping his clothing on the foot of his bunk, Mia disappeared leaving Zane confused. It was day 264 of year 7204, and already it felt like the Monday it was. For a brief second, he thought of returning to sleep, but the memory of the odd dream came back to him and he jumped up to get dressed.

His bed and Mia's were set in the small second room of their home. It was the same room Zane's mother had slept in, the same room Mia had grown up in, along with her parents before her.

The house was larger than most in the Piper's hub; two rooms meant they had space for a proper bedroom. This allowed them to use the other room for cooking and eating with room for Mia to conduct her business of selling clothes.

Despite its size, it did not allow Zane much privacy. He did have a whole corner to himself, one he filled with his inventions. He also had some books, manuals and instructional guides that littered the small shelf above his cot.

Mia had made the room feel larger by placing the furniture against the walls. Warm handmade quilts covered the beds while a patched curtain hung between the two beds for some privacy. The curtain was usually pulled back during the day to give them more room to move about.

Right now, however, the curtain was drawn shut as Zane dressed in the clothes Mia had handed him. He had a quick second to notice she had handed him his best shirt, but after shrugging with indifference, he buttoned it up. As he was clasping the last button Mia's words came back to him. "Guests?"

Curious as to who would be visiting them at such an early hour, Zane glanced again at the clock on his chest plate as he clipped it on over his shirt. Six twenty flashed on the panel as he gave a huge yawn.

Who would be visiting this early? He wondered as he bent to find his shoes. He found one under his cot, but the other seemed to have disappeared. After rummaging around in the small room, he found it behind the chair Mia hung her bathrobe on then quickly placed it on his left foot.

After running his hands through his thick curly black hair, he gave another yawn and headed into the outer room. But when he saw the guests, he stopped dead in his tracks. Panic set in as he saw the two large official looking men sitting on Mia's quilt covered soft chair.

Each man held one of Mia's breakfast biscuits as they glanced up at him. Their dark suites gave away their stature and Zane had a fleeting thought of being dragged away from his home before the biscuits had even been finished.

This was it; they had finally discovered he had been down in the pipes when the man had died. Zane was sure they were here to arrest him.

As his heart raced in his chest, he continued to stand in the doorway and stare at the men. After a moment, Zane realized both men were smiling. This caused him to blink in hesitation. The smaller of the two stood and smiled as he cleared his throat.

"Well, come here boy." The man said and using his free hand, waved Zane into the room. "You must be Zane."

"Zane, come here." Mia scolded as she too waved him into the room. "These men are from the Academy."

"Mathew Carlson, Financial Advisor to the Academy"

The smaller man clarified. "This is the Enrollment Advisor, Vince Tomson."

As Zane sat next to his grandmother, he stared at both men in confusion. The Academy? Thoughts of Mitch flashed in his mind as Mathew Carlson sat once again on Mia's sofa.

"I don't understand." Zane finally said as he turned to look at Mia.

"Zane, these men are here because of a donor." Mia replied and patted a hand at his hair in an attempt to get it to lay down. Zane was glad she hadn't licked her fingers first as he quickly sat forward and studied the men again.

The one called Mathew had thin glasses perched on his very straight nose, his small eyes squinted at Zane. Zane felt Mathew's smile was genuine as it reached his bright blue eyes. The other man, Vince had a more forced smile on his face. Zane thought it was as if he would hold his judgment on Zane until he proved himself. Dark eyes studied him while he held Mia's biscuit with two fingers, still untouched.

"A donor?" Zane asked as his eyes moved from one man to the other.

Again, Mathew cleared his throat before he began. "Yes, we have had a considerable donation, from a private, anonymous individual of course. This donor stipulated that the donation was to be received only upon your enrolment in this year's Level one classes." Now Zane saw speculation cross over the two men's faces, but Mathew continued politely. "As soon as we received these instructions, we proceeded here to collect you. You see, classes started over fifteen days ago, so the delayed start might cause you some difficulty, but your rooms and equipment have all been arranged."

"Excuse me?" Zane asked as he gapped at the two men. "I don't understand. You are telling me that someone paid for me to attend the Academy?"

The very idea that these two men where here to take him to the vast school two hubs away, and not drag him to prison instead was something Zane's sleep muddled mind couldn't comprehend. If both men had turned into the robots he had dreamed of, he wouldn't have been too shocked.

"There is a stipulation, however, that clearly states that the large donation would only be provided upon your enrollment, what you do at the Academy is up to you, but yes." Mathew replied as he politely placed the uneaten biscuit down on the platter set before them. "All details have been taken care of, which means we came to take you back to the Academy, today."

"But," Turning to Mia he saw her face pale a little as she looked back at him. He felt so young all of a sudden, almost vulnerable. He wasn't sure he could go to another hub without his Grandmother. She had always been there for him, raising him, keeping him safe. "But what about my grandmother?"

"There were instructions that she continue to keep your credits, but she is to remain here. Students aren't allowed to bring their families." Vince said with a small sneer of his upper lip.

"She keeps my credits?" Zane asked as both men stood there in his front room.

"We, I mean the Academy will be denied the full donation if you reject the offer." Mathew said and Zane saw a little panic in the man's squinty eyes.

"This donation," Zane stated as he too stood and studied the man's eyes. "It is large?" When Mathew cleared his throat one more time, Zane had his answer. Smiling, he nodded and looked down at his grandmother.

"Why don't you sit down again and tell us everything this donation includes." Mia said with a polite smile.

THE SPECIFICS of the donation were then outlined for both Zane and his grandmother. The donation had included an allowance that consist of housing, clothing and all supplies. It also specified that Mia continue to get Zane's daily credits, despite him not living under her roof during his school days. It was explained that if Zane rejected this gift, that the Academy was also out the large donation. A donation amount that neither men cared to mention when asked.

Mia requested that both men to wait while she and Zane discussed this unusual offer. After taking Zane back into the bedroom she had a quick, yet quiet discussion with him.

"You must go!" Mia said urgently, her clear blue eyes shining with excitement.

"I know, but what about you?" Zane asked, concerned for the only family he had ever known. "How will you run your deliveries?"

Giving a wave of her hand, Mia shook her head. "I will start charging higher delivery fees, this may prompt people to come themselves to get their clothes." She said with a wave of her hand. "But this opportunity you cannot miss!" She hissed and bent to retrieve one of her delivery bags.

Taking Zane's extra pair of shoes, his two pants and three shirts he had on the shelf, she placed them in the bag as he studied her. When she reached over and took the halo of his mother and placed it in the bag, she turned to look at him.

"You will be safe." She urged as she took a deep breath. "You will study, won't you? Take this opportunity seriously and do me proud?" Tears lingered in her eyes as she looked at him.

"Yes." Zane said and smiled at her. "I will."

"Then write to me, every day!" She urged as she bent to find other things to stick into his bag.

Thirty minutes later Zane following the two school Advisors down the path leading to the tram platform. When they got there, it wasn't the tram waiting for them but an Electrical rider or E-rider.

Zane, who had never seen a private E-rider, found himself sitting behind the driver and Vince's seat while Mathew sat next to him on the soft cushioned chair of the back seat.

"Tell me Zane, what interests you?" Mathew asked as Zane tried to get a better look at the E-rider's steering gears.

"What? Oh, anything and everything mechanical." Zane answered and turned his attention to the man beside him. "I invent things. Useful things."

Mathew seemed interested as Zane told him of his inventions. Zane caught Vince glancing over his shoulder several times when he showed Mathew his enhancements to his chest plate. Somehow, this conversation reminded

Zane of the one he had had several days before with Adam.

"What else have you invented?" Vince asked, interrupting Zane's thought of the old man.

The trip took longer than Zane thought it would. He was used to traveling the pipes, a more direct route, one traveled at a high speed on his rail rider which had him traveling under the Primer's hub within minutes. However, above the tunnel levels, it appeared there was no direct route, and the E-rider didn't go as fast as his rail rider did.

The tunnel leading to the main hub was direct, but when their E-rider emerged into the vast dome of the Primer's hub, their travels slowed. Zane didn't care, he was so engrossed by the vision of the Primer's hub that he forgot to continue his conversation with the two school advisors and fell into a silent study of his surroundings.

The sight of the vast city that sat within the Primer's hub drew an excited exclamation from him. Vast tall buildings arose from the ground, shiny white metal glinted in the overhead white lights while bright green plants and trees grew from each level's terrace, draping down the tall buildings.

Several E-riders and a large amount of people littered walkways both on the ground and above on high walkways made of glass. Several bridges spanned the spaces between the tall buildings which were also covered by trees and people.

When their cart stopped for traffic, Zane saw that everyone near them wore new clothing. Bright colored clothes, new shoes and even hats were seen on the people who walked past them. Some had bags and cases while a few had small children dressed similar to them in tow.

The air that pumped out of the vast vents along the lower part of the dome's walls seemed to pump out air faster and far fresher than what came out of the vents below in the tunnels, or even in his home hub. When they passed a pathway corner Zane saw a water fountain and almost fell out of the E-rider. He had never seen water used for anything other than drinking or washing.

When they finally reached another tunnel, Zane craned his neck and glanced back at the massive dome while trying to get one last look. As the tunnel's lights blinked on and off, he thought about all his prior travels under the massive hub. If he had known what sat far above his head, he would have tried to reach the main level years ago.

He thought the wonders of the Primer's hub could not be beat, however when they emerged into the Medical and University hub, he realized he had been wrong. This hub appeared to be as grand as the main one.

It held less tall buildings, instead there were far shorter, odd-shaped buildings. Large fat buildings were set on either side of the dome while taller ones were set in the dome's center. One large main road led down the hub which seemed to separate the buildings, one side had E-riders lined along the front of each building while the other side seemed to have only people milling about.

"Over there are the medical facilities." Mathew said and pointed to the buildings with all the E-riders. "Over here are the dorms and academy buildings." Now he pointed to the buildings with students walking to their classes. "Dorms are lined according to levels. Since you will be starting at one," Clearing his throat again Mathew continued. "I mean you are a Level one student; you will be housed near those classes. You will start in a dorm with several other students, until you obtain level five."

"If you obtain level five, then a separate dorm room will be provided to you." Vince interjected and Zane saw another small sneer form on the man's lip.

"You will start classes tomorrow; your schedule is with your dorm's advisor." Mathew pulled out a small tablet and after clicking several settings found the information he had been looking for. "Ah yes, Taylor will give you the map and schedule. All of your equipment and clothing has been placed in your cube already."

"Clothing?" Zane asked and turned to look at Mathew.

"Uniforms are to be worn to all classes." Mathew said as his small eyes glared down at Zane. "No chest plates are allowed in classes. Also, any missed classes will be marked against you and tallied up at the end of each level."

"What does that mean?" Zane asked as he worried filled his mind about being asked to leave if he missed a single class.

"For you, nothing. For others, they will be penalized, and their parents will be charged for each class missed. But I must warn you, each level obtained requires hard study and determination. If you wish to rise above your current level, you will be required to pass the level's tests. Each student is allowed two chances to pass. If they fail the second time, the student will be finished with school."

Their E-rider stopped before a tall fat building as Mathew finished his instructions. Several shinny windows shone down from above while a few students wearing black pants and grey uniformed tops walked by.

Some students were Zane's age, while others seemed to be as old as twenty years, some carried large books while others had tablets.

"This is your dorm. Taylor can be found on the third floor in the Advisor's room." With this Zane was handed his bag. As he climbed off the E-rider, Mathew smiled at him once more. "Welcome to the Academy."

The E-rider sped away as Zane was left to himself. Turning, he studied the ten-story building and felt for the first time in his life alone. Unsure of himself, of his capabilities had a fleeting thought of his friend Mitch. Maybe he and Mitch would end up in the same classes? Taking some comfort that he might find a friendly face here at school; he climbed the three steps into the building and found the stairway.

He had never seen a E-lift, so he climbed the steps up to the third floor instead. The Advisor's room was the first door he located, and he found Taylor easily. The dorm advisor was a tall sixteen-year-old boy in his fourth level. Tylor had short black hair, orange freckles covered his face, but the smile he flashed Zane was genuine. His blue eyes were filled with curiosity when he saw Zane's blue lighted chest plate.

"Are you from the Pipes?" Taylor asked quickly. "I never met a piper."

Unsure if this was a bad thing, Zane kept quiet as he was led into a vast room that he would share with three other boys. Since Zane had arrived during classes the room was currently empty, but Taylor directed him to his cube. This turned out to be a bed surrounded by a short desk with a wardrobe against one wall which helped separate the spaces.

His school clothing filled the wardrobe and new shoes lined the bottom. Books and a new computer and tablet were sitting on the desk with his name plated on each item.

"Dinner is served in the kitchen dorm, that's two building over to the right, wear your school clothes to prevent any confusion, also you will need to get your ID picture and tag." Taylor advised and handed Zane a small map. "After you change, you can go to the administrator's office for that. Take an E-rider if you find one, otherwise you have to walk across campus."

"Take an E-rider?" Zane asked as joy filled him.

"Sure, they're for student use, but I'll warn you now, if you damage any, they will add the damages it to your tuition."

With this, Zane was left alone. Wanting to shed his Piper's clothing quickly, he found the school pants and belt fit him. It would take him some time before he got used to the stiff shirt, which buttoned in the middle and had a high collar with a single white triangle on it, no doubt indicating he was a level one student.

Once dressed, he studied his reflection in the odd mirror hanging inside his space. He looked different and wondered if his long, unkept hair would be an issue. Unable to change that now, he took Taylor's map and set off to get his ID and tag, whatever that was.

He hoped he could find an E-rider, he wanted to try driving one before too much longer. This thought had him smiling as he exited the building.

EDUCATION

He had located a single E-riders two buildings down, but unsure how to turn the rider on, he sat in its front seat for a while until he grew concerned about his time. After scanning the many buttons and levers, he gave a deep sigh in defeat.

"Next time." He promised the cart and after patting its odd steering wheel, leapt from the machine. After consulting the map, he raced off in what he hoped was the right direction.

According to the map, the Administrator's office was near the dome's outer wall, away from the connecting tunnel. Taylor had been correct, it was quite a way from the dorm building, but Zane was used to running everywhere, there were no E-riders in his hub.

While he traveled, he had a fleeting thought of his rail rider and wished he had brought it. Maybe some modifications could allow him to ride the pathways instead of rails? With plans of a new wheeled rider in his mind, he finally located the right building and stepped into the clean office.

A young lady of around twenty sat behind the tall desk just inside the glass doors. Long dark hair was tied neatly at the base of her small head while deep brown eyes looked up at him as he entered the building. A smile immediately formed on her face as he walked up to her desk, her dress was grey, but she had tied a slash of red around her waist which matched her lips.

"Ah, you must be Zane." She said and stood to walk around the desk. Zane saw that she wore shoes the same color as the belt and lips.

"Yes." Unsure how this woman knew him, he stood there hesitantly and studied her.

"You must be here for your ID. Most students already have theirs, and since I was told you would be arriving today, I made a guess. I'm Sarah." She smiled again as he continued to stand there silently. "I see Head Dean Dickson would like a few words with you first."

Unsure if this was normal, Zane found his palms growing damp as he followed Sarah down a long hallway. Images of smiling students flashed from several halos hung on the walls, all the images showed students holding books with the vision of the Academy behind them. They wore the same uniform Zane was currently wearing, but he saw an array of triangles on their lapel, red, green, and even a golden one indicating their achieved levels.

They passed several closed doors until they reached a double wide door at the hallway's end. Sarah gave a soft knock and after receiving a quick answer from inside, opened the door for Zane.

"Head Dean, I have Zane Noman here for you." Sarah

said and gently pushed Zane into the room before shutting the door behind him.

Panicked and unsure if he should proceed inside the room, Zane studied the space first. He had never seen real wooden beams and wood floors before, only the harsh metal of his hub and his home. Large bookshelves covered one wall and a thick brown rug sat under a massive desk set in the room's center, behind which sat the Dean.

"Well, come on in." Head Dean said with a gruff deep voice.

Stepping further into the room Zane's eyes were instantly drawn away from the Dean towards movement behind the man. The entire wall behind the Head Dean was covered with a variety of clocks. Large, polished clocks, some bigger than Zane, others tiny intricately carved and smaller than his hand. Some clocks had pendulums swinging back and forth, it was their movement that had caught Zane's eyes. Each clock was different than the one next to it and all showed the time of sixteen hundred.

Turning his eyes from the array of clocks, Zane found two black eyes studying him. Head Dean was a rather round man around sixty years. Bald and pasty colored, Head Dean made up for the lack of hair on his head by having a thick beard covering his entire face.

"Sit." The order came out as a bark, one that Zane quickly followed. As he sunk into an armchair covered in mauve, the Dean's eyes followed his movements. "Tell me, why are you here?"

Confused and panicked, Zane felt his jaw drop open as he stared back at the man.

"Um, she said you wanted to speak with me?" Zane squeaked as his mind emptied of the receptionist's name.

"No, I mean here at the Academy." Head Dean explained and leaned forward over his desk. "This donor, very strange business. But I have also been contacted by the Primer, highly unusual." Zane felt that the Head Dean hadn't meant to speak aloud the last statement, as the man quickly stood and faced away from him. After facing the clocks for a few minutes, Head Dean turned back towards him. "Have many friends in the pipes?"

Confused and unable to keep up with the man's array of questions, Zane just looked at the Head Dean with wide eyes.

"Um, no. Not many." Zane said with a shake of his head.

"No matter, no matter." A thick hand waved in the air between them as he rounded the desk to stand in front of Zane. "Take heed, this establishment needs the donation your enrollment will provide us. But we do not tolerate any trouble," When the man leaned closer to Zane, he saw the dark eyes narrow. "Have you been in trouble before?"

Unsure how he should answer, Zane remained silent. When the Head Dean continued to stare at him, Zane quickly responded with a short. "No."

Several more seconds of silence followed before the man either saw the answer he was looking for, or felt he had intimidated Zane enough. He nodded once and walked back to sit behind his desk.

"Very well, Sarah will take you to get your documents in order." Waving his hand again at Zane, he felt he had been dismissed and quickly stood and walked to the door.

However, before he reached for the knob, Head Dean spoke once again.

"We will be keeping our eye on you."

Zane quickly made his way back to where Sarah sat, a smile on her face. "Come, we will get your halo and all your codes for you."

Zane had his photo taken, his fingerprints printed and even spoke his full name into a machine that then spat out an odd-looking card. The card had his full name, hub, and photo on the front.

"You will use this for entry into the library and several classrooms." Sarah stated as she showed him how to scan the card for access to the doors.

Since she seemed genuinely nice, Zane asked her how to start the E-riders after she had finished all her instructions. She only showed a little shock that he didn't know, but quickly agreed to walk out and show him how to start the closest one. She also showed him the odd peddles that controlled the E-riders.

Confident with his new knowledge, he sat behind the U-shaped wheel and took off. It didn't go as fast as his rail rider, but he felt a rush of excitement as he puttered along the unknown pathways. Thoughts of exploring the entire hub flashed in his mind, but they were quickly squashed. He had other, more important things for today.

With the excitement of discover and exploration in his mind, he was distracted from his driving and almost hit a recycle shoot. Trying to avoid this, he skimmed a rather large bush before he got the hand of the steering. After that, he remained focused on his driving.

He found the E-rider just thrilling and took his time exploring the Academy side of the dome. He didn't venture onto the medical side of the dome but vowed to himself that he would explore that area later.

Hungry after his travels, he scanned the time and decided to park the E-rider in front of the building Taylor's mad indicate was the Kitchen building. Since there were several E-riders littering the sidewalk in-front of the building, Zane felt confident it was dinner time.

The kitchen hall was a low, long building with wide double doors and many windows. Expecting processors that could be programed to spit out food, Zane was shocked when he saw a line of students waiting along a large counter that held hot, fresh food.

Mia had cooked all his meals for him, she had cooked them using the food provided by the processor. One could order plain protein and white grains, which were cheaper and costs less credits. Then you would take them home and use the products to make many different meals. Most families from the pipes saved credits by asking for bulk items instead of asking for a single meal which usually costs more.

Here at the Academy, it appeared they strived to save credits too. Beyond the line of students, he saw protein cakes, wheat patties, corn substitute, the green of veggie cubes along with the variety of vegetable orbs. He also saw sweet cakes and oat cookies which made him smile. Mia wasn't here to limit his intake of sweets.

Grabbing a tray, Zane moved into the nearest line and waited his turn. He saw both boys and girls lined around him, each wearing the black uniforms and ID tag. Some were younger than him, distinguishable by their smaller size, while most appeared older.

He knew from his conversation with his dorm advisor,

Taylor, that there weren't many kids from the Pipes. In fact, he wondered if he and Mitch would be the only two kids from that hub. Thinking of Mitch, he quickly scanned around the room, hoping he would see his best friend. Not spotting his friend, he turned his attention back to the girl in front of him. She was a foot shorter than him; her dark blond hair was tied up and he saw she kept wiggling her left foot as if she were nervous.

When she looked over her shoulder at him, he saw big brown eyes quickly glance his way before she turned to face the front again. The fast glance he had seen, showed a pretty girl about his own age. She had a cute nose and full lips which had been set with worry when she had glanced at him.

Zane saw the foot tap double time after she turned back around. Before they had reached the long food filled table, Zane heard two loud voices and saw the girl cross her arms defensively and duck her head.

"There she is!" One deep voice said as a high-pitched laugh followed the statement.

"So, you decided to bless us with your presence, *princess.*" Came a deep sneer. "Slumming, are we?"

The tone and words had Zane's back teeth on edge as he turned and saw three boys approach the line. The tallest boy had wavy blond hair with a large toothy grin as he immitted another high snicker. The center boy was a foot shorter than his companion; his long face was set in a sneer as his grey eyes briefly glanced Zane's way. With a quick dismissal, Zane knew the boy wouldn't give him a second thought as he turned his attention back to the girl. The third boy had dark skin and black eyes with hair about Zane's length. Large ears stuck out of the dark locks and his smile was pulled to one side as he excessively nodded his head.

"Weston, leave me alone." The girl moaned and stepped forward in the line, no doubt hoping the three would not follow.

Another loud giggle from the blond boy had everyone around them staring. Zane knew from his own experience that some kids liked to pick on others different than themselves. Especially an easy target, like a boy who had no father.

Growing up, Zane had been a daily target to the kids in his hub. He had been called names, pushed and shoved and even beaten up a few times. Most of these incidences had happened before he had turned ten, before the kids his age had been allowed down in the pipes with their fathers. Before ten, kids were taught by their mothers, taught to read, write and do simple math. After the age of ten, they graduated to an age where they followed their father or an uncle down into the tunnels to learn how to maintain the pipes that kept ECHO alive.

It was at that time Zane had realized the vast difference between him and the other children. He had been teased, but until the age of ten, the implications of not having a father had been lost on him. Until no man had called him forward to teach him the essentials of working in the pipes. Without a teacher or guide, he was denied all access to the tunnels where the pipes were which kept his home alive.

For Zane, denial of something only increased his yearning for that thing. Realizing he was not allowed in the tunnels during the day; he had taken it as a challenge. Sneaking into the pipes at night had been his secret, for four years he explored and discovered to his young hearts content.

Seeing another person being teased never sat well with him, he knew it was this fact that had formed his friendship with Mitch. Despite their age difference, their bond was stronger because they both felt the harsh sting of disapproval from others in their hub.

"What no private chef for you?" The dark-skinned boy's taunt drew Zane back to the dining hall and had another giggle from blondie.

Narrowing his eyes, Zane studied the three and saw quickly the leader must be the boy standing in the center. His grey eyes continued to be focused on the girl and he had a half smirk on his face while his companions teased her.

Confident they were leaving him alone; he too quickly turned his attention to the girl. What he saw, had his shoulders slumping in frustration.

Tears threatened to fall from her big eyes and when her shoulders started to shake Zane felt an odd little tug beneath his chest. Knowing he couldn't stand by and let them continue to tease her, Zane stepped forward, immediately drawing their attention to him.

"Well, I see you found a boyfriend." Weston said with a snicker. "Where did you find him? Down in the pipes?"

"I am sure you meant that as an insult, however without the pipers, you and your friends here wouldn't have any toilets to drink from." Zane stated with his own sneer, he knew how to deal with bullies. "Are these two even potty trained?" Seeing the shock and anger cover the boy's face, Zane knew his insult had been quickly received.

"What did you say?" The boy asked as he took a threatening step towards Zane.

"What? Don't you understand English?" Zane replied, speaking slowly as if talking to a child, as he stood his ground. "I can speak slower if you need me to."

He was ready for the punch, those who found words no longer damaging, always turned to the more mundane abuse of physical threats. As Weston's right fist pushed through the air at him, Zane took a quick step backwards, twisting to the side. Keeping his right foot forward he jutted it sideways, so the boy's forward movement caused him to trip over it.

When Weston was face down on the clean tiled floor, Zane turned to see the dark-skinned boy rushing at him. Zane had a second to push the girl out of the way, then felt the boy's body ram into him from the back. Taking the weight of the fall, he twisted his shoulder around and rolled onto his left side. He felt a nasty pop, but quickly entangled the boy's legs with his own as his arms came up and locked around the kid's midriff.

Zane knew from experience that one couldn't fully punch a person that was too close to you. This was a lesson he had learned the hard way early in life. Keeping the boy within his grip, he turned to ensure the others weren't trying to aim kicks at him.

Seeing the blond tall boy standing there dumb struck, Zane rolled with the currently struggling boy and ended up on top of him, making sure to keep his legs tangled while his arms clamped around him tightly. Not willing to let go, he smiled down at his foe, adding insult with his cocky grin he turned to look up at the girl who was standing there with her mouth wide open. After sending her a wink he smiled at her.

"These *boys* weren't giving you trouble, were they?" He asked, emphasizing the word boys, her brown eyes were wide with shock. When a smile formed on her lips, he turned his attention back to Weston who was still sprawled on the floor. "I think you owe her an apology." Zane stated as the boy moved to stand while the one within his strong grip continued to struggle.

"What is this!" Came an authoritative voice causing Zane to quickly release the boy, who then quickly jumped up and raced out of the room. No doubt before the professor had a chance to push through the crowd and see his face.

Upon gaining his feet after the fight, Zane had been scolded by a Professor Bradson, a shorter man with thinning grey hair and eagle eyes that studied him.

The lecture had been long and winded ending with the professor writing down Zane's name. Since Zane had no idea what punishment they inflicted here, he turned back to the food line after the professor had marched off. He found the girl with the large brow eyes gone, no doubt she had fled sometime during the professor's scolding.

'She hadn't even stuck around to say thank you.' Zane thought with a shake of his head.

"Not even here one day and you're already in trouble." Taylor said with a shake of his head as he followed Zane to his dorm room later that evening.

After giving Taylor a quick shrug, he headed towards

his cube. When he saw the room was no longer empty, he stopped in his tracks.

"Introductions." Taylor said as he slapped his hand on Zane's back with a laugh. "This skinny one's Evan. He is from the fixer hub, knows how most of everything in this building works and can show you around if you get lost."

Zane studied the black kid of 16, he appeared to be built much like Zane. Evan had a friendly face which already had a small amount of black hair growing on the tip of his chin, his hair stood mostly from the top of his head and was buzzed near his ears. He nodded with a smile as he returned Zane's gaze.

"Next, we have Miles, he doesn't talk much, tends to sulk if you ask me." Taylor said as he walked Zane further into the room.

Zane saw a dark-haired boy around his own age who tried to look bored. His wild long hair gave Zane the impression he didn't have a mother or grandmother who constantly nagging him about haircuts. When dark eyes turned away, as if finished with the assessment, Zane shrugged and followed Taylor further towards his cube.

"Lastly we have Rafe. This kids a Primer, but despite that, he seems to know his stuff." Taylor said with a laugh.

"Takes one to know one." Rafe said with a grin. Zane saw Rafe's eyes wink with amusement as he turned his brown eyes towards Zane. Rafe had to be about sixteen, his square jaw gave him a rugged look that Zane always hoped he would one day achieve.

"Hey, my mom came from the fixers, so I claim both hubs." Taylor replied with a smile. "There, you're all introduced. Now, get ready for bed."

Zane moved to his cube after Taylor left and after

taking his shoes off, looked up to see three pair of eyes looking at him. It was Rafe who spoke first as he walked closer to Zane's cube.

"Did I hear you were already causing trouble?" He asked as Zane sat on his own bunk.

Another shrug of his shoulders caused Rafe to step closer. Speculation and doubt filled his eyes as he puckered his lips in thought.

"Probably just got lost." Evan said with doubt as he walked away and sat on his own bunk.

"Got in a fight." Zane mumbled as he watched Rafe turn quickly on his heels.

"Who'd you fight? Didn't you just get here?" Rafe quickly asked as he neared the end of Zane's bed, his hands on his hips in disbelief.

"A boy named Weston and his gang were trying to tease someone." Zane said and saw Evan and Miles stand and then walk over.

"You took on Weston?" Evan asked with shock as Rafe held up a hand to silence him.

"It was Breanna they were picking on, wasn't it?" Rafe asked as he kept his brown eyes on Zane.

"I don't know her name, long dark blond with big brown eyes." Zane said and saw Rafe nod his head. "Then yeah."

Unsure if he was amongst friends of Weston, Zane now worried he might have to defend himself once again. Moving to stand up, he was interrupted when Evan started to laugh.

"Hope you bloodied them good." Evan said as he walked closer to Zane.

"Would have loved to see that, did you kick em hard?"

Rafe asked as he smiled down at Zane.

Zane told his story of the fight, embellishing a little for his three new roommates. He was hesitant to tell them he was from the pipes, but when Evan asked about the piper hub, Zane guessed Taylor had already told the three where he was from.

"I've only been to the pipe hub once with my dad." Evan said as his dark eyes grew wide. "We Fixers don't get called there much."

"That's because we learn to fix whatever needs fixing ourselves." Zane said with a shake of his head.

"I was told that." Evan said as he leaned closer to Zane. "Smart bunch from what I gathered, heard tell they can even do coding when they need to."

Another shrug had Rafe laughing. "You don't give much away, do you?"

"Not much to tell." Zane said as all three boys looked at him with disbelief.

"That's not true." Miles said, his bored look remained on his face, but speculation was in his eyes.

"How does a piper afford the academy?" Evan asked.

"Easy, I can't." Zane said and leaned back against the metal headboard on his cot. He found it odd having a real conversation with kids his own age, a conversation that didn't involve answering questions about his unknow father or why he wasn't working in the pipes. But as the talk turned to his unknown donor, he grew uneasy.

"What do you mean?" Rafe asked.

"I can't afford it, neither can my grandmother." As soon as the words were out, Zane regretting letting the three know he lived with neither of his parents. Being an orphan usually gave him unwanted sympathy. Instead, the three boys looked at Zane with speculation and doubt, looks Zane was used to and dread started to build in him. Would these three boys treat him differently if they knew his past?

"Then how are you here?" Miles once again spoke up.

"Anonymous donor." Zane finally replied when he realized this answer was the truth. After seeing confusion in all three faces he decided to explain to them about his day. After completing his story, Rafe and Evan had lots of questions that Zane was unable to answer.

No, Zane didn't know who the donor was and didn't really care. This education would allow him to rise above the level he had been born into. Something he would have never been allowed to do, not on the small credits he and Mia earned, even with her sewing job.

After receiving no answers to their questions, all three boys moved off towards their own bunks. Zane was unused about talking to anyone other than Mia or Mitch that he worried for a time about their conversation, would telling these three his story result in them to seclude him?

With these thoughts still in his mind, Zane found three pairs of pajamas in his drawers, each with his initials sewn into the lapel. After changing into them, he hung up the uniform and found his personal bag still in the bottom of his wardrobe. When it gave a small squeak, he jumped with shock.

His two-way talker was emitting static. Grabbing it quickly he held the off button until he locked himself in the bathroom.

"Mitch?" Zane asked after running the sink water to cover the noise.

"Zane? Zane is that really you?" He heard Mitch's young voice and instantly smiled.

"Yeah!" Zane said with a wide grin.

"Zane, did you boost the signal? How am I getting you, and you sound so clear too?" Mitch asked.

"That's because I'm at the Academy, just like you!" Zane replied as the line grew silent. "Mitch? Are you there still?"

"Zane, you're here? At the academy?" Speculation filled Mitch's young voice now.

"Yeah, there was a donor who paid for my way. And before you ask, I don't know who my donor is." Zane replied and was once again met with silence.

After a few minutes, Zane asked if Mitch was still there.

"Yeah, just thinking. Zane, have you told anyone else about what you saw in the pipes?"

Confused by Mitch's question Zane looked down at the TWT held in his hand. All of a sudden, his odd conversation with Head Dean Dickson came back to him. After going over the conversation in his mind again, he finally answered his friend.

"You know I told Mia, but she wouldn't tell anyone. Why?" Again, silence met his question. "Mitch, what is going on?"

"Zane, we might be in trouble." Fear filled Zane at his friend's words. "I didn't tell anyone, I swear, and I never will. But Zane, three days after I got here, I was called to the Head Dean's office. Zane, the Primer was there, the actual Primer, Kasher. She asked me about my life in the Pipes. Zane, I didn't tell her about you, not even when she asked me if I had any friends. She was looking at me with such a hard look I feared she already knew about you. Then she asked me if I had ever been down in the pipes."

Sweat trickled down Zane's back as Mitch continued to talk. Once again, the Dean's odd behavior and questions popped into Zane's mind.

"Zane, she had my map. The one I drew you. I think you lost it down there near, near the man."

LESSONS

Zane didn't sleep much that night, the bed was comfortable, but his mind kept him awake. He heard the soft snoring across the room and couldn't tell if it was Miles or Evan who kept the odd rhythmed sound going. It didn't matter, that night Zane thought of all the mysteries which he found himself surrounded by lately.

Who had paid for his school? Why had they paid such an expensive cost for him to come here to the Academy? Why him? Who was Waltson? And more importantly, who was the dead man down in the pipes?

When he finally fell asleep the dead man's voice echoed out at him.

"You don't own me, you may own others, but not me."

"I know your secrets!" Zane heard the high pitch of the woman's threat.

"I know yours." The man growled in response.

Zane awoke with the sounds of the loud ping still echoing in his ears.

On the 265th day of the year, Zane started his classes.

Level one students all received the same education, despite any prior training they may have received from their own families. The same level, the same uniforms, and the use of first names only ensured all students were treated equally.

To Zane, this presented security along with a fresh start. He had always been eager to learn. Mia had never had to force him to read his lessons. But when he had reached the extent of Mia's own learning, Zane had sought another type of knowledge.

To Zane, the hands-on experience netted him much more than he had expected. Running rampant in the pipes had given him more knowledge than even he could have dreamed.

He had learned all about the pipes with their twists and turns, their release valves and joints. He knew when a pipe was starting to fail by its appearance, its color and yes, sometimes the smell. Fresh or scrubbed air flowing into the tunnels would always cause him to stop. This was something you couldn't learn by a book.

His nightly explorations also allowed him to discover the electrical conduits that ran under the hubs. He had learned quickly of the charge stations and what their gages meant.

Now, being taught more, and being taught by actual professors caused a euphoria like feeling in him. For the first time in his life, he found the vast world of knowledge stretched out before him, all within his grasp.

Rafe and Evan were eager to help him to their first class, they called it Base class. They led him down the path, three buildings behind their dorm and one to the right, to their first class as Miles trailed reluctantly behind. Zane, still unsure how to act around other boys his age kept quiet as his new friends talked around him. He was pleased when they included him in their conversations but still remained guarded about himself.

The building was a vast metal structure that had over ten stories to it and was larger than any building Zane had yet been in. The entry's double doors opened to a vast room with two winding stairs leading up to a second level. Zane was sure his home and five more like it could fit inside the lobby area but said nothing as he followed his new friends down the hall.

When they entered a tiny room that held a row of shiny buttons, he watched curiously as Rafe hit the button with the number four on it. It took all his power to hold in a scream as the doors closed and the room started to move.

Eyes wide with shock, Rafe must have seen Zane's reactions and quietly told him the elevator was quicker than taking the stairs. Giving his new friend a nod, Zane told himself he was going to investigate elevators when he had a moment alone that night.

Professor Luthier led Base class, her skinny figure was dressed in a black robe, which Zane found out later was the typical uniform for the professors. She also had a grim expression on her wrinkled face. Long grey hair tied on the top of her head made her appear taller than she really was and Zane marveled that not a single hair stuck out from the bun, it was as if she kept each in place by sheer will.

She nodded at Zane as he entered the large room and marked something down on her chart. Without sending a greeting to him, she pointed to a corner desk as she continued to study him with her steel blue eyes.

The classroom was a wide room that sloped upward and had raised seating at the back. Narrow walkways in straight rows led up as desk and chairs spilled out from the main rows. The room was already halfway full, and more students piled in behind them.

Zane held in his emotions when he spotted Mitch two rows in front of him. Their conversation the night before still fresh in his mind he thought back to Mitch's statement.

"She had my map." Mitch had told Zane the night before. *"Zane, she asked if I knew how a map I had drawn could end up in the pipes."*

"What did you tell her?" Zane asked as his heart beat quickly.

"I told her I had lost that map, that I only drew it from a book because I liked to trace pictures and maps." Mitch stated and Zane could hear worry in his friend's voice. *"Zane, she had the Academy doctors check on my legs. I think she thought I was the one in the pipes that night. You know, the night..."*

"I know what night Mitch." Zane's mind unwillingly returned to the dead man's face. He remembered the man grabbing his arm so tight. He thought about the whole event and realized that when he pulled free from the man's grip, his pocket must have been ripped. That's when he must have lost the map, a map he hadn't even remember until Mitch had mentioned it.

"So, what did she do after they confirmed you are cripple?" Zane asked, fearing his friend's answer.

"She asked me if I had given the map to any of my brothers or sisters, maybe even a friend." Mitch's voice squeaked a little

over the handheld device. "Mitch, I think she's looking at my family or for you."

"You didn't tell her about me, did you?" Zane quickly asked.

"Of course not!" Mitch sounded hurt. "I would never! But Zane, she is looking for someone, someone close to me who may have been carrying the map. She knows someone was in the tunnel with the dead man. Zane, this is why we have to pretend we don't know each other."

"Why?" Zane asked, both shocked and confused by his friend's words.

"Don't you see, if we know each other from our hub, she will hear about it and Zane, I worry she will find you." Mitch said quietly. "She scares me."

With Mitch's words still echoing in his mind, his eyes slowly slid right over Mitch, whose crutch was leaning against the desk, his green eyes focused on the book before him. It was as if he didn't even dare to look at Zane or their secret would be out.

After taking his seat, Professor Luthier started, Zane found her class highly informative. She used an actual book, not an electronic book, and proceeded to give the class information without interruption. She talked the whole hour of class about the hubs, their functions and even some of their history. Using his electronic note pad, Zane had four pages of notes before she even paused or look up from her book.

"Tonight, you will need to read pages six through twelve in chapter two. This week's test will be given at zero eight hundred, sharp!" This must be her normal dismissal, because no sooner had the words left her lips when several students stood to leave.

"What class do you have next?" Rafe asked as he neared Zane's desk.

Zane told him he had Government with a Professor Ricker and then Electronics afterwards.

"You and I have two classes together, but Evan has this next one with you. He can take you there, then you have one with Miles." Rafe looked at Miles with a grim look and nodded to him.

When Miles gave a huge sigh, he nodded his head which caused his long hair to fall around his thin face. "Fine. I'll keep an eye on him."

Rafe seemed pleased with this as Zane turned and looked at him. "I don't need looking after." He said and tried to cross his arms over his chest defensively.

"Not what I meant." Rafe said quickly and held his hands up trying to calm Zane. "It's just better that you're surrounded by friends, what with your argument with Weston yesterday." Using only his eyes, Rafe turned and looked to the back of the room as Zane stood from his chair.

Turning, Zane saw that the boy from yesterday's fight was standing at the far back of the room. Weston and his two buddies were there, all three had sour expressions on their faces, no laugh came from the tall blond boy today.

Knowing when he was outnumbered and fearing an ambush in unknown territory, Zane conceded to "being looked after" by his new bunk mates.

As they turned to leave, Zane saw the pretty girl from yesterday ahead of them. Her long dark-blond hair was tied in a single braid today and he saw a tall girl with black hair walking next to her. He watched her head off in the opposite direction from the one Evan took him.

As they walked, Zane's thoughts turned towards her, Rafe had called her Breanna. Why had Weston and his cronies been teasing her? Why hadn't she thanked him?

His teenage mind speculated, and he thought of asking Evan about her, but decided now wasn't the time as they neared their next class. Maybe later he would ask Rafe about the girl.

THE WHIRL WIND of classes that day amazed Zane. After Base class, he had Government with a Professor Ricker, a short lady with a ruler straight bob of hair and little glasses that kept slipping down her nose when she looked away from the electronic board.

This class was in a newer building covered with bright metal walls painted white. The floors were tiled, something Zane hadn't seen before, and handmade rugs littered the lobby with bright paintings on the walls. The classroom was on the main floor and was half the size as his first class's room.

Then he had Electronics taught by a Professor Bradson, a short balding man who reminded Zane of several Forcers he knew. He spoke in short barks and scolded several students for not paying attention. Screens sat on each desk and the walls were littered with posters of cable diagrams. Zane recognized several pictures, some of ULTAC processor cables and another which broke down a printer's function.

He found himself already burdened with homework for that night well before lunch time. When lunch did come, he was glad for the break. His three bunk mates turned out to be helpful as most of his classes were in different buildings and across campus from each other.

They ate lunch together and Zane saw Mitch again. Seeing his best friend eating lunch alone, sitting at a large table with no one near him, broke his heart. But he had sworn to Mitch that he wouldn't approach him, that he would pretend not to know him, for both their safety.

Miles kept quiet during lunch but both Rafe and Evan talked excessively to him. Rafe had storied of the main hub that Evan would laugh at or add to as they both seemed to know several of the same places in the Primer hub.

"Where were you raised?" Zane asked Miles after Evan had talked about the fixer hub.

Miles looked shocked at the question then quickly turned his expression to a bored look again. "Here." He finally said. "Parents are both doctors."

"Really?" Zane asked excitedly. "I haven't had a chance to explore that half of the hub, is it different than here?"

But before Miles could answer, the buzzer sounded signaling the end of free time. Next, he had Building Code class. Rafe walked him to the pyramid shaped building that seemed to point upward towards the dome's ceiling. Green vines grew on the outside walls with round windows set here and there. Instead of individual desks there were tall tables that sat four students each. Here the walls were covered in prints of buildings, each a replica building found inside the Academy hub.

Professor Spencerson started the class by asking each student to describe one building in their home hub in writing. He asked that the assignment be turned in before the end of the class and explained that they would spend the rest of the week going over details of each building.

"Tomorrow I will have you explain the positives' of the building and the next day its negatives – how it's builders failed in its design." Professor Spencerson said, his tall form gliding around the room in his black robes. When the professor neared Zane's desk, he saw the man wore bright red shoes that made a soft 'pft' noise as he passed. The noise caused Zane to chuckle silently to himself.

Two more classes were left but Zane felt like he had already spent four days in class not six hours. Miles helped him find the computer lab for coding. On their walk across the campus, Miles had quietly told him that Computer coding was his favorite class. After this statement, however, Miles frowned and gave a quick shrug of his thin shoulders as he led Zane into the vast room.

Computer switches lined the walls and two rows of desks, each with their own monitor, sat in the center of the long skinny room. The professor, a small mousy man with very thick glasses led this lesson.

Zane thought Professor Davison odd until he started his class, then Zane knew the man was strange. Numbers and codes spewed from the Professor's lips as fast as words and Zane felt his head swim with confusion.

Unsure what his assignment was, or how he would eventually pass the class let alone the rest of the hour, Zane studied the electronic book displayed on his computer which sat before him and fell further into puzzlement.

Maybe computer coding wasn't for him? He thought and turned to see Miles looking at him.

"Don't worry, I'll catch you up tonight." Miles whispered quietly and clicked a button on Zane's keyboard that had his training book turning to the correct page.

"Thanks." Zane whispered back and tried to find where they were on the page, feelings of inadequacies mixed with his overwhelming frustration. Feeling lost and confused by the end of that class, Zane was pleased when he discovered Evan outside the lab waiting to take him to their next and last class.

"Don't worry," Evan told him with a smile on his face, his white teeth shining brightly as his dark brown eyes winked at him. "Everyone gets lost the first day in Professor Davison's class."

Evan's words helped ease some of Zane's frustration regarding the class, however, his worry about his own abilities remained.

The last class of the day was an environmentalist class. Professor Danson was a grim tall man. His silver hair was combed back from a wide forehead and there was an easy smile covering his face. Zane learned in this class about the recyclers and the vast machines that were used to keep ECHO supplied with all the basic human needs. Zane learned twenty new things before the class was over that day and had yet more homework.

He saw Mitch was in this class too and again felt the urge to talk to his best friend. He also saw Breanna in the classroom. Her dark-haired friend was missing and when he had passed her desk, she looked up quickly at him and smiled. But just as quickly as her smile flashed at him, she had ducked her head back down.

Walking back to their dorm after the last class, Rafe and Miles joined Evan and Zane long before they reached the door to their building. Knowing he had tons of schoolwork, Zane worried that the two hours before dinner wouldn't be enough time.

"I could show you some of the coding if you want." Miles suggested as they entered their room.

"Thanks, I think I need help." Zane replied and followed Miles into his cube's area.

Miles tried to help explain the three pages the professor had covered in their class. When he found out that Zane didn't even know the basic words for coding, he stopped his review and instead showed him the code sheet with all the technical terms.

"Once you learn these words and their definitions, you'll have an easier time with coding." Mile advised Zane.

Zane spent the next hour on his other assignments until Rafe interrupted his studies for dinner. The four of them headed over together to eat the meal, each talking about their school day and laughing and joking with each other.

When they arrived at the kitchen hall, Zane found it hard not to stare at the number of students inside the large room. Sliding walls had been opened on either side of the main eating area making the entire room appear more like a long corridor instead of a square room. Additional tables and chairs were set about and even a few couches littered the areas near the windows. Each chair and table appeared to be crowded with students.

Zane knew his home hub wasn't the largest in ECHO. And the pipes had no location large enough for all of his fellow pipe inhabitants to gathered in one location. His home hub didn't even have a center square for large gatherings.

"Breakfast and lunch are served at three different times; this allows students to eat according to their individual schedules. But dinner is only served at one time, six to eight." Rafe supplied when he saw Zane's astonished face when they neared the shortest line for food.

"If you show up after eight, you don't eat." Evan said with a smirk.

Trying to look at everything at once, Zane soon was distracted when he saw the pretty girl from the day before approaching him. Breanna's big eyes were focused on him and her lips were in a frown as she walked up to him.

"Excuse me." She said with a slightly husky voice. "Can I speak with you?" She asked and looked to either side of him where his new friends stood. "Alone?" She then added.

Feeling his face heat a little, he nodded and followed her away from the food line toward the opposite wall. She aimed for a section of the wall which had no tables or students near, then turned to study him again.

Under her gaze, his face warmed up, feeling mortified and worried he was bright pink, he shuffled his feet as she continued to study him. When she smiled a little, he felt the heat creep up towards his ears.

"I wanted to thank you." He must have looked confused or shocked because she quickly continued. "You know, for what you did yesterday."

Finding his voice wouldn't work because his mouth had gone completely dry, he quickly cleared his throat and tried to speak. His tongue wanted to stick to the top of his mouth and his mind had gone blank of every thought or words he should respond with.

"It was nothing..." He finally croaked out after a minute of silence.

"Yes, it was." She quickly interrupted. "No one else stepped forward yesterday, but you did." When she placed one of her hands on his sleeve, he felt the heat from her touch spread up his. "Don't you see, the whole hall knew what those boys were up to, but you alone stepped forward. And all by yourself too." She shook her head and looked down as she took her hand from his arm. "I'm ashamed that I didn't stick around to thank you. I should have..."

"No, I mean, I understand." Zane said quickly as her big brown eyes looked back up at him.

"Did you get penalized much?" She asked and must have seen confusion in his face because she continued. "Will they charge your parents much, for the fight?" She asked.

Shrugging his shoulders, he shook his head. "They didn't say."

"You mean the professor didn't tell you. Please, if you find out, let me know. I will pay the fee." With this statement, she gave him a smile again. "I'm Breanna by the way."

"I know, I mean I asked my friends." He said quickly as she continued to study him.

"And you are?" She asked with another smile as if she knew a secret he didn't know.

"Oh, yeah, I'm Zane." He had almost said his last name but luckily, he stopped abruptly and then filled the following silence with a smile.

"Zane, nice to meet you. Again, thank you for your

help." She gave him another smile and turned to leave. "I'll see you in class."

With that last promise, she was gone. She quickly disappeared into the crowd of students which was walking past him. Feeling foolish as he continued to stand and stare after her, Zane finally turned and walked back to his friends. When he got to them, they had already reached the front of the food line. After they all dished up with piles of food which consisted of protein loaf, veggie orbs and tons of sweets, they sat at an empty round table.

"So, what did Ms. Primary want?" Rafe asked as he stuffed a rather large bite of bread in his mouth.

"What?" Zane asked, confused by his friend's words.

"Breanna, what did she want?" He repeated.

"Oh, she wanted to apologize and thank me for stopping Weston from teasing her yesterday." Setting his fork down, Zane studied Rafe who was still stuffing his mouth with bread. "Why did you call her that?"

"What?" Rafe asked around another large mouthful of bread. After swallowing, he smiled at Zane and rolled his eyes. "Oh, Ms. Primary? Well, Breanna is Primary Kasher's daughter. Didn't you know that?"

With Rafe's words, Zane felt his heart skip several beats. Blast it, she was the Primary's daughter! The very person he and Mitch were trying to avoid. If Breanna found out Zane was from the Pipes, then Primary Kasher might find out about his friendship with Mitch. What if she found out it was Zane in the pipes that night? That it was he who had been there when the man had been killed.

His stomach gave a big lurch as his mind filled with dread at all the possibilities that could befall him if he were discovered. Prison being one of these worries, he felt his appetite disappear.

"Aren't you going to eat?" Evan asked, his dark eyes on the pile of sweet bread which sat upon Zane's plate.

When he shook his head, Evan quickly stabbed one slice of bread from Zane's plate and stuffed it in his mouth.

Filled with his own thoughts, Zane sat at the table while his friends ate his food and talked around him. One thing was sure in Zane's mind, he had to talk to Mitch. Face to face.

PROBLEMS

*M*itch refused to meet Zane that night, or the next. In fact, two weeks passed before Mitch would even allow Zane to bring up the possibility of seeing each other during their nightly talks over the two ways. They had taken to talking over the TWT each night, filling each other in on their day and school activities.

Mitch's private room was closer to the main hall, it was in a building that house professors, not students. He had also been given his own E-Rider to travel to meals but found there was always a professor willing to join him for the jaunt to the kitchen hall, so he was never left alone. Mitch's private room was only six buildings down the path from where Zane's dorm room was. But to Zane it felt like his friend was as far away as another hub.

"I don't care what you say, we still have to pretend not to know each other." Mitch stated one night after Zane had finally told him about his odd meeting with the Dean. "I think the Primary has several of the professors reporting to her." Mitch stated, worry filled his young voice. "If they see me talking to you, we could both be in trouble."

With the fear of being discovered still in their minds, both boys continued to pass one another in the halls and classrooms as if they didn't know one another.

Mitch had also cautioned Zane about interacting with Breanna further, but Mitch couldn't explain why it bothered him so much. Zane tried to avoid Breanna, but it appeared since her show of appreciation to Zane, she must have found it easier to talk to him.

Zane was both pleased and perplexed that in each class they shared she went out of her way to sit next to him. Since he still found himself tongue tied around the pretty girl, it was hard for him to discourage this.

Most of the time she did all the talking while he sat quietly by and occasionally nodded in agreement as his palms sweated. He was sure there was a goofy smile on his face and reminded himself that next time he would discourage her from sitting next to him. This pledge to himself was strong, until the next time, when he would completely forget his resolution.

His bunk mates thought his reaction to Breanna was funny and took every opportunity to tease him. He found it easy to take this type of teasing as Evan and Mitch also pestered Rafe for his "relationship" with a pretty red head girl named Asher.

Zane worked to complete his school assignments each night and found his struggle in Coding class difficult. However, with Mile's help, he thought his grades in this lesson were acceptable. He got his best grades in Base class and Environmental class but struggled in Government and worried he wouldn't pass the first test.

To his surprise, his scores were decent when they were posted a week after the tests. All scores were sent electronically to the student, along with their parents which is why Mia sent him a private message via a message pod the next day. When he heard her voice over the machines small speaker telling him she was pleased with his scores he realized all of a sudden just how much he missed her.

He knew the message cost Mia a whole day's credits and quickly sent her his own message, using his school funds, telling her he missed her too, and he would be coming home for Launch day for a whole week. He also urged her to save her credits and not send another message pod but an E-letter instead.

He hoped the remaining three weeks before the holiday week would pass quickly. With studies, school assignments and friends, he thought the days passed too quickly.

Each night he and Mitch would talk over his TWT, but their conversations had to be pushed later into the night because of studies.

Finding time away from his friends was also difficult. Rafe and Evan loved to pass the nights talking and joking. Sometimes they would go out of their dorm building and throw Rafe's disc around. The flat hard plastic disc held several stickers on it and at first Zane had a hard time catching it because he smashed his finger. But after several days of practice, he was pleased that he was able to catch it without injury when it was thrown at him.

Rafe and Evan told him about the disc tournaments that were held in the main hub. They spoke of large open areas which were designated for the sport. A sport that was practiced by most kids in the Primer hub. All three of his friends were shocked when Zane told them his hub didn't have any games or sports.

"Work and more work are what we have." He told them as they threw the disc around in front of their building.

"What do you do for fun?" Miles asked with shock on his face. It appeared even the dower kid found it shocking to not have games to play.

Zane was on the verge of saying he explored the pipes when he remembered it was a secret that he had been down in the tunnels. "I invent things." He blurted out instead. This prompted them to ask about his inventions and before he knew it, he had promised he would bring his rail rider back from his holiday stay.

He knew he would have to retro fit it with a wheel before he brought it back, as currently it only rode on the rails down in the pipes. He couldn't bring an invention back that would prove he had been sneaking into the pipes at night.

Two nights before students were allowed to return homes for the holiday, Zane got a slip from the Academy's Dean confirming a private E-rider would take him back to the Piper hub for the holiday.

Since it said nothing about a car taking Mitch to the same hub, Zane quickly asked his friend that night during their private talk about his return trip to the hub.

"I got a note saying I would be allowed back for the holiday, but it didn't say anything about a private rider." Mitch told him. "I'm worried Primary Kasher will take me, just like she picked me up and brought me here."

"Surely she's too busy to pick you up." Zane said shocked.

"Remember, her daughter is here at school too, maybe she will use that as an excuse. Zane, several professor's keep asking me about friends from home, even friends I have here. Everywhere I turn I find their eyes on me." He wasn't sure if Mitch was exaggerating, but his friend's words struck fear in him none the less.

"We need to meet." Zane urged once again as his thoughts turned to his friendship with Breanna. She had recently started eating meals with Zane and his friends, something he had tried to discourage, but found he still couldn't form any negative words towards her when she was near him.

Rafe's girl Asher had also joined them along with one of Breanna's friend, a chocolate skinned girl from the fixer hub named Delany. Without Zane knowing how, his small group of new friends had expanded and grown.

"We can, but after we get home." Mitch's words had Zane's heart beating quickly. "I think I can get away the second day home."

"On Launch day?" Zane asked.

"Yeah, my family always celebrates early. It leaves the rest of the day open. I can tell them I want to take a walk."

"Where can we meet?" Zane asked quickly.

The plan was simple. On the second day home, the day the people of ECHO celebrated the Launch of the ECHO program, Zane would meet Mitch near the back wall of the dome. It would be close to Mitch's home so he wouldn't have far to walk. Since most families sat down to eat the festive meal around thirteen hundred, they hoped the pathways would be empty. Mitch still insisted they keep their meeting secret from their family members and made Zane promise to not tell Mia too.

Zane struggled emotionally as he changed out of his school uniform and back into his Piper clothes. His home cloths had soft material and they were well sewn, but it wasn't the Academy uniforms which allowed him to hide his origin hub. He secretly hoped that if any students saw him, they would think he was from the fixer hub, or even maybe the Printer hub.

Realizing quickly that he was ashamed of his home hub caused a different emotion to fill him. Ashamed of his shame in his home hub, he squared his shoulders and finished getting dressed.

With luck, maybe no one would see him as he quickly made his way down to the private E-rider. He wasn't shocked to see Mathew Carlson, the Academy's financial advisor, sitting in the back seat. He was, however, glad Vince Tomson, the enrollment advisor, was missing on this ride.

He and Mathew had a wonderful conversation of lessons and grades that cheered Zane up as the E-rider traveled out of the Academy hub and down the connecting tunnel.

Zane still marveled at the wonderful view of the Primer hub when they passed along the wide streets, but he didn't turn and glance back when they neared the tunnel that would lead him home. When they drew to a stop inside his home hub, he was shocked to realized he had deeply missed it. The familiar smells of meals cooking, the sounds of young children running along the paths and even a blinking bulb that had yet to be replaced brought him joy.

He told Mathew that he didn't need to walk him home. It took some convincing, but finally the man agreed to let Zane walk home by himself.

When Zane walked in the front door of his home, Mia immediately flung herself into his arms and cried. She kept touching his face and telling him he had grown, something she was quick to measure and note down in a special book she had ever since he had come home from the hospital.

"Two whole inches!" She clucked and immediately started making new pants for him since he had grown too tall for his old pare.

AFTER FITTINGS and then a special dinner, Zane itched to run over and see Mitch. He knew his friend had urged him to keep their relationship a secret but being home wiped the worry of threats far from Zane's mind.

Instead of running over to see Mitch, he resolved to spending the evening working on his rail rider. Using his school pass, he logged onto his tablet and found schematics for a message pod. He was hoping to fit the rider with an air lift kit like the message pods had. But after spending a half hour looking at the drawings of the gears and levers which allowed the square machines to fly, he finally gave up. He would have to settle for attaching a wheel to his rider, for now.

With visions of one day flying around on his little rider still in his head he spent several hours working on the wheel adjustments. After removing the clamps that attached the rider to the rails, he spent a whole hour debating over which wheel to use.

In the end, he used the fattest one he had, an old twenty-meter tire which sat between the two small foot platforms. Most of the tire's rubber tread had worn off, but the tire still held air. Balance wouldn't be an issue, as the fat tire would help and he had added a self-adjusting gear crank. At least he hoped he could balance, he did worry about hitting bumps, but figured he could try out the new wheel rider tomorrow.

When he finally fell asleep that night, he dreamed of large wheels bouncing around him as he tried to study for the computer coding exam. When the dream turned dark, as it usually did, and a flash of the dead man's face appeared Zane awoke. At first, he thought he was at school, but smelling his familiar home and hearing Mia snore softly from across the room, he snuggled down in his comfortable bed and quickly fell back to sleep.

Mia made his favorite breakfast, protein links with wheat cakes, the next morning. He ate two portions and after helping clean up, spent his morning on the finishing elements of his rider.

When the time came for him to meet Mitch, he thought he would give the rider a test run. Zane quickly found out that riding on a flat rail was different than riding on a bumpy walkway. Each time the wheel hit a grove Zane was almost bucked off.

He stopped twice to make minor adjustments before he felt more stable on the metal platform that sat on either side of the wheel. When he arrived at their meeting site, he was pleased to see Mitch already there.

Mitch, his crutch holding him up, looked very pale as Zane stopped and picked up his rider and flashed his friend a smile.

"Quickly, back here!" Mitch said and waved Zane forward as he ducked behind the nearest building.

The dome's wall was feet away, and a small shed had been built right up against it. Mitch walked to the corner of the shed and after looking around, opened the door and waved Zane in.

"What are you doing?" Zane asked when Mitch quickly shut the door behind him. He saw Mitch's chest plate's lights flash on as his young friend looked up at him.

"Zane, we're in trouble." Mitch whispered; his voice squeaky as he grabbed at Zane's arm. "They know. Zane, they know about you."

"What?" Zane found his own voice's pitch raised as he grabbed Mitch's arms in return.

"Well, not about you, at least I'm not sure. But Zane, my mom talked to the Piper's Advisor just last week."

"What do you mean?"

"Zane, I think she told Advisor Jeffson about our friendship." Mitch hissed; his eyes wide with fear.

"Oh." This news sunk in as Zane took a deep breath. "But that was a week ago, if they knew about me wouldn't they have questioned me by now?"

Mitch shook his head as he released Zane's arm. "I don't know. I think they would have to report the information to the Forcers first."

"Mitch, in Government class I learned that each hub Advisor only meets with the Luminaries once a month." Zane said thoughtfully.

"Zane, that's under normal situations. With the death and reward, I bet they are meeting once a week. And if the

Primary has been asking me questions, I bet she's been asking people in this hub questions about me too."

"Mitch, I never meant to get you into trouble." Zane said as he looked down at his young friend, all of a sudden acutely aware of their age difference. "I never thought my exploring the pipes would ever lead to this. I shouldn't have dropped your map."

"I know you didn't mean any of this. What I don't know is why the Primary is so interested in finding you. Are they trying to pin the murder on you? Or maybe just on any Piper?" Mitch leaned back and Zane saw his eyes look around as he thought.

"Maybe they aren't even looking for the real killer? Maybe we should have come forward right away, told them what I saw and heard?" Zane urged as a coldness settled inside him.

"No," Mitch said quickly. "No. You have to keep quiet. The last thing we need is to be suspected of murder. Until the actual killer is found, we have to remain quiet."

"What have you told the Primary?" Fear still filled Zane as they stood hidden in the tiny shed.

"She asked about my family, if one of my siblings could have taken the map. I told her I think I had lost it while walking in the hub, not at home, but I'm not sure she believed me."

"And what did you tell her about friends?" Zane asked.

"That was easy. I told her most of my friends went into the pipes during the day. This is true because all my friends are my brothers and sisters." Mitch shrugged his small shoulders and smiled up at Zane. "Of course, she asked if I had known of anyone creeping around the pipes at night. I told her the truth, that no one I knew creeping around the pipes." Again, his youthful smile flashed. "I don't think you ever snuck, did you?"

Zane smiled when he replied, "No, never crept, I always went in and rode my rider around as bold as I could. There was never anyone there to sneak past." Finding Mitch's smile contagious he laughed before another thought hit him. "Mitch, did you enter the lotter?"

"Of course. Mom has had me enter my papers for the past five years. She has never heard of a Piper getting picked, but since my school grades are the highest for level one students, I figured I had won fairly." Zane saw speculation cross Mitch's face as he looked back up at him. "Zane, what if..."

"I'm sure you're correct," Zane quickly interrupted. "you won it based on your entry." Zane said convincingly.

"But what about you?" Mitch said and once again his young eyes grew wide in the blue light of Zane's chest plate. "What if this donation was only done because they found out about you?"

This question had been on Zane's mind since the day he woke to find the two school advisors sitting in Mia's living room. Thinking of it now, he came up with the same answer he always did.

After shaking his head, he told Mitch his conclusions. "No, Mathew told me that if I rejected the offer, that the academy wouldn't get a single credit. Whoever my donor is, they want me to finish as much schooling as I am able. Why would my donor want to send me to school if they meant me harm or thought me a killer?"

"I thought the same thing, but Zane, we don't know

who the killer is, only that it's a woman." Mitch said with a shaky voice.

"And her light was green." Zane said thoughtfully.

There still hadn't been any official word on who Zane had seen die that night. If the forcers and the Primary knew, they were not giving the name to the public.

This was cause for concern and also speculation. Was the dead man a high advisor, someone of importance in the government?

The only thing they knew about the man was he wasn't a Piper. After the word of a death in the pipes got around the hub, the first thing the Piper's advisor, a man named Jeffson, had done was take a count of all pipers. When the count had been done, it was discovered that not one piper was missing.

Both boys had used this news to continue their investigation into who the man could have been. But without knowing the man's identity they could only speculate on his cryptic message to Zane.

Again, the boys found their questions unanswered when it came to finding this Waltson. Neither knew any man named Walt, nor his son. They guessed that this person wouldn't be in their hub and Mitch had taken to scanning ECHO's registry trying to find anyone with that name. He had found over a hundred people with that last name but without a first name, they couldn't narrow down the search.

They talked about their questions, speculations and concerns for several more minutes before Zane realized he would be late for Mia's special Launch day meal and started home.

Mia always made her special protein hash with flat

cakes and sweet rice patties for afterwards. Since this meal was one of Zane's favorites, he quickened his pace on his rider when he neared home.

His stomach gave a loud rumble as he pushed the door opened and called out to Mia as he dropped his rider just inside the door. His smile was still on his face when he turned and found two men sitting on Mia's couch. The first man he knew, Piper Advisor Jeffson, a skinny older man who currently had his long frame tucked into Mia's couch almost looked comical. But the second man had Zane's mouth going dry and his heart beats increasing.

Davis Elliotson, the Primary's personal Advisor sat across from Mia. His face set in a frown as he looked up at Zane.

LAUNCH DAY

*D*avis Elliotson slowly stood from Mia's couch when Zane entered. Mia rushed forward to greet Zane, her face pale with worry, but her mouth set in a firm line Zane knew meant someone was in trouble.

"Zane," Mia stated and placed a protective arm around him. "Advisor Jeffson and Elliotson have paid us a visit and have been asking many questions."

Fearing his voice wouldn't work, Zane turned his eyes from the two men to Mia's. Her blue eyes squinted a little and she smiled down at him as she squeezed him in a tight grip.

"I have told them you were just out visiting several friends. Friends you have missed since you've been at the Academy." She walked Zane over to the remaining chair and after pushing him down, sat on the chair's arm, keeping close to him. "Now gentlemen, what other questions did you have for me?" The words were spoken sweetly, but Zane knew that tone. Mia usually used it right before he was grounded after doing something wrong.

"Well, we were hoping to talk with Zane alone." Davis Elliotson said as he sat back down and turned his eyes back to Zane. Zane thought the man meant for his smile to be charming, but there were far too many teeth showing, in his opinion.

"I'm afraid that's not possible." Mia replied just as sweetly. "You see, I'm his guardian. All questions will be asked with me present."

Davis nodded once but kept his eyes on Zane. The man must have been about thirty, setting his youthful face in a frown he leaned forward a little.

"It has been presented to Advisor Jeffson that you may know something about the crime that took place down in the pipes on the night of the 257th day, at around twenty hundred hours."

Zane felt his throat contract as he tried to swallow. His palms grew sweaty as he looked back at the man, unable to think, let alone answer Zane could only return the man's gaze. When Mia's laughter broke the silence, Zane took a deep breath, not even realizing he had been holding his breath.

"Someone is playing a joke on you two." Mia finally said after her laughter quieted.

"Excuse me?" Davis said with a frown as his dark brows lowered over his eyes. "Joke?"

"Why yes, you do realize that Zane isn't allowed down in the pipes during work hours, let alone at night. He has had no one to train him regarding the pipes. No one that took up his training who is related to him, that is." Mia said as she waved her hands about and made a show of pouring more tea for the two men. "Why someone must be playing a joke of you."

"And why is that?" Davis asked, his tone firm, but Zane heard a hint of doubt in his voice.

"Why, surly you know?" Mia said, her voice sounding shocked. "Why Zane's last name is Noman. He wouldn't know the first thing about the vast tunnels down there." Mia shook her head as if in disbelief.

"Are you saying you know nothing about the crime?" Davis asked and tried to look past Mia at Zane. Mia once again made a big show of trying to serve the men a piece of her rice patties.

"How would he?" Mia once again interjected, successfully drawing the men's attention away from Zane and back to her.

"He may have heard something?" Davis said and was quickly interrupted by Advisor Jeffson.

"His name was given to me as a possible witness." Jeffson stated, his thin lips turned down as his grey eyes remained on Zane.

"Witness? And where was this crime done?" Mia quickly asked as she stood and completely blocked Zane from the two men's view.

"The pipes." Jeffson answered.

Again, Mia's laughter sounded. "The pipes!" Mia's voice rose as she stood there and looked down at the two men. "So, a boy who has never set foot inside the pipes, and has never been trained inside the tunnels, is supposed to find his way in and out of there?" Mia's head shook as she spoke.

"I have it on good authority that Zane has traveled inside the pipes several times, each night in fact." Jeffson said as he stood to confront Mia. "Regularly." He quickly added in a hiss.

"We need to know if you were down there." Davis said as he too stood. "If you were, we need to…."

A loud buzzing interrupted Davis before he could finish. Quickly the man reached in his pocket and Zane saw another frown cover the man's face as Davis pulled a small black device out. Zane had never seen a personal communication's device before, so when Davis looked down at the fancy black box Zane's eyes went wide.

"Davis." The man stated after hitting a red button on the top of the box.

"I am recalling you." Came a deep voice out of the box.

"Sir?" Davis replied after once again hitting the red button. "Who is this?"

"Waltson." The single reply had Davis's face turning pale while Zane's heart skipping several beats.

"Yes sir." Davis said quickly and turned to Advisor Jeffson. "We are done."

Neither man said a word as they both turned and quickly walked out the door, neither pausing to even shut the door. Both advisors didn't even glance backwards nor gave an excuse for their quick departure.

"Mia!" Zane hissed as she rushed forward and quickly shut the door.

"I know, I heard it too." Mia said as she turned quickly to Zane. After giving him a hug, he felt her body start to shake.

"Mia, Waltson!" Zane said and realized it wasn't Mia shaking but him.

"It's ok. At least for now." Mia replied. "How did they find you?" She asked and gave Zane another squeeze then she moved to clean the plates from her table as if she wanted to remove all evidence that the men had been in her home.

"It was Mitch's mom. He thinks she had gone to see Advisor Jeffson while we were at school." Zane provided as he sat again in the chair.

"That woman!" Mia states as she stopped her cleaning to look down at Zane. "I'll bar her from buying from me." With this, Mia turned and finished cleaning her front room as if the two men had left a foul odor in her house.

"Mitch was worried she would do this, but I never expected to see Davis Elliotson here." Zane said and sat staring off into space.

"Zane, why is the Primary's advisor involved?" Mia voiced a question Zane had no answer to.

"The real question is who is Waltson?" Zane finally said, his worry and confusion mixed together as Mia continued to clean.

AFTER THE HOLIDAY BREAK, Mathew once again returned in the private E-cart to drive Zane back to the Academy. Zane had changed into his school uniform well before the cart arrived, wanting to return to school in his uniform and not the Piper clothes he had.

Thanks to Mia, Zane now had several new pairs of pants but still felt more comfortable in the uniform. Mia had used his unused food credits to buy newly printed material and presented Zane with these clothes as a present for the holiday. Besides two new pants three shirts and new underwear and socks, she also sent him back to school with a stack of homemade flat cakes.

On the drive back to the Academy, Mathew talked about the next quarter and what Zane could expect. Zane listened, but his mind was still on the mystery of who Waltson was. They had just passed beyond the Prime hub when Zane thought of asking Mathew if he knew who Waltson was.

"What's the name?" Mathew asked and turned to look at Zane.

"Waltson." Zane replied and studied the man as he thought intently, his brow furrowed, and a hand scratched absently at his cheek.

"No, never heard of a Waltson. Do you know his first name?" Zane shook his head and felt deflated when Mathew sighed deeply.

"Well, if he attended the Academy, you could always check the register." Mathew's words gave Zane some hope, maybe Mitch could cross reference his list with the school's.

The campus was chaotic when Mathew dropped Zane back at his dorm building. Students of all levels were returning from holiday, most had large bags flung over their shoulders, one or two had trunks and Zane saw one girl with a cart full of bags.

Rushing in with his small bag of clothes, which also contained a bag of cakes, he realized he was the first back to the room. Rafe's cube was empty, but when he looked closer, he saw signs that Miles had been staying in the dorm during the small vacation. His bed wasn't made, and Mile's coding books were sitting on the edge of his desk.

After taking out the cakes, Zane shoved his new clothes in the bottom of his wardrobe and pulled out his school tablet. Sitting down at his desk he pulled up the program Mathew had told him about.

'The Academy Register' was under the intro about the Academy. Zane found the search program and typed in Waltson.

Feeling a course of adrenaline, he watched the machine purr as it searched for the name.

When over forty different men named Waltson appeared on the screen, he found it hard not to be discouraged once again. He attempted to run the name based on years and found that only twenty of the men were still alive. He saved the list and thought of sending a copy to Mitch but worried about the contact being traced or intercepted. When he heard voices outside the dorm, he shut down the system as his bunk mates all came in laughing.

Well before dinner that night all of Mia's cakes had been eaten and Zane's wheel rider had been inspected and then tried by all of his friends. Rafe rode the wheel rider well, even Evan could stay on the rider longer than Miles who struggled riding two feet before he would jump off.

"You have to use your stomach muscles to keep yourself upright!" Rafe said with a laugh as they watched Miles jump off the rider.

"He doesn't have any muscles, that's his problem." Evan's laughed.

Before they called it quits that night, Miles could ride the wheel rider ten feet. He didn't quite have turning, but Zane was sure with more practice, his friend would get the hand of the rider.

When he and his friends arrived at Base class the next day, they heard a hushed silence sweep over the room as they entered. Professor Luthier wasn't in the room yet and the immediate silence confused them.

"Well, if it isn't the Piper!" Weston mocked as the room fell silent.

Zane immediately felt the blood drain from his face as Weston who stood at the back of the classroom smirked at him.

"Hay, Noname! Did you spend the holidays down in the sewers?" Manny, the blond boy, said with a loud giggle.

In his humiliation, Zane would have rushed from the room except his friends came up behind him and surrounded him. He felt Evan pat his back once as they glared up at Weston.

"Leave him alone!" Came a high-pitched voice from across the room from where they stood.

Turning, Zane saw Breanna get to her feet. Her face was red, and her small fists were clenched as she faced the three bullies.

"Oh," Weston sneered. "your girlfriend wants to defend you; does she know you don't have a father?"

"Probably didn't want to claim him, too ugly." The dark-skinned bully named Omar scoffed as he flashed his teeth at Zane. For some reason, Omar's smile reminded Zane of Davis Elliotson's toothy grin.

"Shut up!" Breanna screamed, unfortunately her scream was still radiating around the room just as the professor came in.

"Miss Bryer! That will be enough!" Professor Luthier said as she came marching into the room. Her thin face set as she peered at Breanna with a frown on her thin lips.

Breanna's face paled several shades as the professor

continued to study her. Zane didn't hear what Weston said next, all he knew was that a low grumble could be heard from Breanna as she turned from the professor and launched herself at the tall boy.

Breanna's clenched fists flew at Weston's nose resulting in blood squirting from the boy's face. Zane stood shocked in his spot as the professor whipped past them and raced up the steps. Luckily, Breanna got in one more solid punch before the professor pulled her off of Weston.

"Miss Bryer!" Professor Luthier screamed as she tried to pull the small bundle of fury from the bleeding boy. "That's it! Report immediately to the Dean!"

At the professor's words, Breanna finally stopped trying to kick out at Weston. She went placid as Professor Luthier finally released her.

It tore Zane's gut apart when he saw tears falling from Breanna's pretty eyes as she walked past him and his friends. Her head lowered after she passed him and remained down as she left quietly and closed the door behind her.

"Probably get a big fine." Evan whispered to Zane as they sat down at their desks, a grin on his face as he whispered, "Totally worth it."

Zane's ears were buzzing during the class. His own embarrassment of being called out for being a Piper and not having a father was nothing now compared to his concern for Breanna. His worry for her increased when he didn't see her at lunch nor in Environmentalist class. His worry that she had been expelled had him asking her friend Delany about her.

"The Dean contacted her mother, but Breanna's still

here." Delany informed Zane at dinner. "She's taking her meal in her dorm, but I expect she'll be back to class tomorrow."

"Did they charge her family much?" Evan asked between mouthfuls of sweet cakes.

"I don't know, but she got an earful from the Dean." Delany replied with a shake of her head.

"She shouldn't have stood up for me like that." Zane exclaimed with a shake of his head.

"She did, and the rest of us would have too if Weston and his stupid friends had continued much more." Delany said with a frown. "I hope she broke his nose."

Feeling embarrassed to be the subject of conversation and the reason Breanna was in trouble, he ate the rest of the meal in silence, his head hung in shame.

That night Mitch and Zane talked only about Breanna. Mitch still wanted Zane to stay away from her, but he did spend several minutes telling Zane how fun it was to see Weston's nose gush blood all over.

"I think both nostrils were bleeding after the second blow." Mitch speculated as Zane smiled into the TWT that night.

"Mitch, how did they find out where I'm from?" Zane asked after a minute of thoughtful silence.

"Probably looked you up on the register." Mitch replied, Zane had the image of his friend shrugging his shoulders. "Everything about students can be found there."

This statement had Zane quickly relaying his forgotten information about Waltson.

"I can narrow that search down if you send me the

list." Mitch stated. "Could you pass me the list tomorrow during Base class?"

The next day Professor Luthier was already in the classroom long before the first student arrived. Breanna was there too, her head down as she studied notes at a desk across the room from where Zane and she normally sat.

"Come on." Zane said to Rafe and the others, who then followed him over to Breanna's corner and sat, surrounding around her.

She glanced up when Zane sat in the chair next to her and returned his smile after he quietly mouthed a quick 'thank you'. She didn't say anything but nodded once and returned to her notes.

His next two classes seemed to drag by slowly. Zane thought Government class was tedious, Professor Ricker's monotone voice droned on about the layers of government which kept ECHO running while the minutes slowly ticked away.

Zane didn't look forward to the essay Professor Ricker assigned. They were instructed to name each high official and do a short bio on the men and women who currently held these high-level jobs. Since they had four days to complete this assignment, Zane only worked halfheartedly on it during class.

Next was Professor Bradson's Electronics class. Zane liked this class, but again his mind wandered as the professor spoke of circuits and conduits that Zane already knew about.

When lunch finally arrived, he and Miles, who had Electronics' with him, made their way to the kitchen hall.

Two paths from the hall they found their path blocked by Weston and his two friends.

"No girl to protect you now Piper." Weston scoffed as Miles dropped his school bag and stood in front of Zane.

"Weston, you'll get charged for fighting." Miles scolded with a shake of his head.

"There are no professors here." Omar said, his toothy smile flashed as he rubbed the knuckles on his right hand.

"Doesn't mean they aren't looking." Miles said with a shake of his head.

"We just want to talk is all." Weston sneered and took a threatening step closer.

"Well I don't want to talk to you." Zane stated and bent to pick up Mile's bag. "Come on Miles." Zane grabbed Mile's arm and tried to pull his friend around the group, however Manny and Omar moved quickly to block their way.

"How are you here anyway?" Weston demanded as he continued to block Zane's way. "With no father I mean. Is your mother a companion? That must be it, is she paying for your way by working?"

Zane didn't remember clenching his fist, he also didn't remember throwing the first punch. Through his anger he didn't feel the shock of the punch when his knuckles sliced open on Weston's front tooth.

When he could finally see through the haze of anger, he noticed that the boy's nose was once again bleeding. Then he was tackled from behind as Omar hit him and wrapped his arms around Zane's knees.

Kicking out once, Zane heard Omar grunt as he tried to roll over onto his back as his hip cried out in pain from where he had landed. He felt a fist hit him in the soft part of his side and bunched his muscles as another one landed in the same spot.

Quickly rolling once again, he grabbed at the fist which was currently heading towards his chest and was able to stop it inches away. Making sure to grab a finger, he then twisted it and felt satisfaction when Omar squealed in pain.

He was reaching back to land a punch in Omar's toothy face when the boy was unceremoniously hauled off Zane. As he watched, Omar's body few away and landed in a large bush four feet away.

Rafe stood over Zane, his roughed face set in anger as his dark brows lowered over his eyes. Zane had a fleeting thought that he never wanted to cross Rafe, because the boy's current stance was very threatening, anger made him look dangerous.

Rafe turned and using his right arm, pulled Manny off the ground, who immediately slumped in the larger boy's arms in defeat. Zane was pleased when he saw Manny's right eye already swollen shut.

"Looks like you two needed help." Rafe calmly stated as he used his left hand and reached to help Zane up. Once Zane had gained his feet, Rafe smiled and released Manny from his grip.

The blond boy slumped down on the ground and took a few deep breaths before jumping up and racing away, not even looking back to see if his friends were following him.

Turning, Zane saw Evan sitting on Weston's back, a smile on Evan's dark face while the bully continued to kick and scream.

"He didn't get hit enough from Breanna; it appears he

came back to get his nose completely broken." Evan laughed and after a motion from Rafe, slowly stood to release Weston.

"Leave Zane alone!" Rafe growled, Weston gave Rafe a glare, but then turned and quickly raced after his fleeing friends.

The four boys stood there and watched the three bullies disappear around a building before bending over and laughing like idiots. Zane's side hurt where Omar had hit him, and his knuckle started aching when he finally stopped laughing.

"Did they hurt you two?" Rafe asked as he sobered up and studied Zane and Miles.

"I split my knuckle, think I cracked Weston's tooth." Zane replied as he rubbed the bloody knuckle on his black pants and turned to look at Miles.

The smile on the boy's face shocked Zane. Miles had a split lip, and an excitement look was in his usually bored eyes as he grinned at Zane.

"Well, you may want to clean up before heading to lunch." Rafe stated with a shake of his head. "We'll save you a seat."

Since no one else had seen the fight, the boys had a hard time explaining their visible injuries to their other friends. Miles tried to tell people he fell, but somehow the rumor that he had walked into a pole was already being spread around the hall.

Zane told people he got his hand stuck in a E-Cart wheel, but since only Breanna asked after his hand, he was disappointed by her lack of sympathy.

"You shouldn't be playing with the E-carts if you don't

know how to work them." She scolded with a disapproving shake of her head.

Zane didn't think Weston's face would ever go back to normal, his nose and lip were swollen for three days, then it turned a deep purple to Breanna's pleasure who thought the boy's injuries were caused by her.

GRADES

For Zane, the schoolwork seemed to be excessive. Each day the assignments and essays grew in number and difficulty.

Base class was by far the easiest. Here he was quizzed on things he had known his whole life. Facts like; the hubs were actual round domes, reaching as high above their heads as they were below their feet. The five perfect circles housed the equipment they used to remain alive for generations.

The perfect Biospheres which housed and sustained those who lived in ECHO. What most didn't know, or see, were the pipes. But since Zane had been sneaking into these tunnels, it was easy for him to know what little they taught about them.

At first, he was shocked at how small Professor Luthier taught about the pipes. He thought the skinny woman was going to cover the basics on all the hub's functions. But when she started going into great detail about the printers he wondered if there were more to come about the pipes later. Maybe in another lesson or another level.

He was disappointed when they moved from the printers on to the recyclers. Confused by the lack of data regarding the pipes, he asked the other boys if they knew.

"Not much to learn about the pipes, those who are raised there take care of them." Evan replied one night in their rooms. "Even the Fixers don't have the knowledge to repair them."

Shocked about this fact, Zane realized his home hub was more secluded than he had previously thought. If he and Mitch were the first Pipers to go to the Academy then how had ECHO and more importantly the Pipes, survived so long?

He wondered if the parent training given by the Pipers were enough, maybe they were more efficient than he knew. Or maybe, he wondered, if the miles of pipes were easier to maintain than he had been told.

Government class was another issue. Here Zane felt the struggles of his lack of formal education. Learning layers upon layers of the government was difficult for him. There was a government official and title for everyone down from the man who opened the door for the Primary, a man named Bill, all the way to a man named Ken who punched the credits through for new residences.

Zane learned about the Forcer's Master Commander, a woman who oversaw all the hub's forcers. He learned about the chain of command for each hub's forcers all the way down to his own hub's six forcers.

Electronics class was less hands on than Zane had hoped. The class had less to do with the circuits and wires used to make his wheel rider than it did with diagrams of color-coded instructions. He found his head hurt after each of these classes and was thankful he wasn't color blind at the end of each lesson.

At least Professor Spencerson kept his Architect class interesting. But even in this course, he was having to learn technical terms that kept eluding him. Words like sustainability, façade and deconstruction all had to be defined and used in assignments correctly.

Zane thought that Computer Coding class was the most difficult. Each day the little professor spouted out numbers as if each student should know what he was saying. Most students kept their eyes on the book or screen as if following Professor Davison's words, to the frustration of Zane. Miles helped him each evening, but even then, Zane found himself losing ground in the class.

The lessons were far beyond his capability and his frustration grew each day as the end of term tests grew near. When test day came, Zane found his stomach refused to settle and the single piece of grain square threatened to return.

During each lesson's test his head swam with useless facts yet the answers to most questions eluded him. Sweet trickled down his forehead making his vision swim until he came across a question that he was confident in its answer. Then his self-confidence grew, and he would proceed with more enthusiasm.

Worried about his first grade of the second term in Computer Coding class, he had Miles open his E-ticket. As Miles opened the link for him, Zane's heartbeat increased.

"89!" Miles quickly said excitedly and gave Zane a grin then a quick slap on the back.

"No!" Zane said before he could think and shook his head. "That can't be right."

Grabbing his tablet, Zane felt a ball of ice form in the pit of his stomach as he read the flashing green number indicating he had passed his latest test. A small buzzing noise sounded in his ears as he looked over the grade, something was wrong.

He knew he had worked hard in his studies, but this subject had eluded him repeatedly. Questions and answers seemed to mix up each time he was in the class. Zane knew he could re-wire an electrical box down in the pipes, had done it several times, but for some reason he found the professor's coding jargon beyond his grasp.

As he stared at the 89 flashing before him, a sick feeling came to him. Was this grade fake? His conversation with the Academy's financial advisor came back to him as he stared at his tablet.

"We, I mean the Academy will be denied the full donation if you reject the offer." Mathew had told Zane while sitting in Mia's front room.

Now Zane wondered if the donation would be denied the Academy if Zane flunked out of a level. Could the donator's restrictions include such a restriction?

Mia had taught Zane to stand on his own two feet his whole life. She had taught him to be proud of who he was, despite his having no father.

"Stand and build your own life." She had told him. *"Don't let others dictate who you are, they only know and see what is lacking in your life, not what you have in here."* She said and with a smile, rested a hand on his heart.

Mia's words and teachings came to him as the green numbers continued to flash before him. Each flash of green seemed to ask him what it was he was made of. Are you a man who would duck your head and continue to live with the unknown, or are you made of stronger stuff? After a short internal struggle, Zane had his answer.

"Miles, what did you get?" Zane asked feeling the icy ball grow.

"I managed to get a 92." Miles replied as his dark eyes studied him. "What's going on?"

Shaking his head, Zane opened the link to his graded test. "What did you get for number six?"

When Miles opened his own test and read the correct answer, Zane's uneasiness grew. His head hurt as he asked for Mile's answers on several more problems. Each time Miles provided a different answer than Zane had provided on his test, yet Zane's test showed his answers were marked as correct.

"What is going on?" Miles asked as he looked over Zane's shoulder to get a better look at his tablet.

"I don't know, but I know where I can get some answers." Zane stated as grabbed his wheel rider then headed for the door leaving his friend confused.

He found Professor Davison huddled over a computer in the classroom, his disheveled hair sticking up as if he had just run his fingers through the grey whisps. The room was empty, but still the light on the consoles blinked on and off as if expecting students any minute.

"Sir?" Zane asked and had to repeat it until the professor heard him and finally responded.

"Ah, yes. What can I do for you today?" Beady little

eyes blinked several times behind the thick glasses, Zane saw the man's eyes struggle to focus on him.

"Sir, I have questions about my grade." Zane saw the man's eyes narrow quickly before he moved to study his computer once again.

"All scores are final." Professor Davison stated and waved a hand dismissively at Zane.

"Sir, but there are several mistakes that weren't marked on my test." Zane urged and walked forward towards the professor. He didn't know why he was here arguing about a great grade one higher than he deserved, but the urge to find out the mystery of why this professor gave him such a good grade was too strong.

"Don't know what you're talking about. All scores are final. Congratulations on the pass." Again, the professor waived his thick little hand at Zane.

"Sir," Zane replied and finally reached the man's side. "These problems were answered wrong." The ball of ice was now growing up into his chest. Why was the professor insistent on his passing grade, when according to Zane, he had failed the test, miserably?

Zane saw the little man's thick chest give a mighty heave and then the small eyes turned to face him once again. "Let's go see Head Dean Dickson, maybe he can shed some light on this conundrum."

With these words, Zane's fear grew. Was he causing problems by questioning his final grade? He knew the grade was wrong, and something in him needed to know the answer. Why had this teacher marked his grade as pass, when clearly, he had failed?

After nodding, Professor Davison stood and led the way out the room and down to the building's front door.

"Where is the cart you used to get here?" The professor's eyes glanced around as Zane cleared his throat.

"Um, I didn't take a E-cart. I used my wheel rider." Zane replied as he held up his homemade wheel board.

"What is that?" The professor's little eyes squinted even more behind his thick lenses as he studied Zane's rider.

"I made it, I use it.." He was about to explain the rider's function when Financial Advisor Mathew drove up in an E-cart.

"Ah Professor Davison, and Zane!" Mathew's face beamed when he saw Zane. "Hello! How is your second semester going so far?" Mathew asked as stopped the cart inches from Professor Davison's toes.

"Ah, Mathew, just the man we need." The professor said as he climbed into the cart's passenger seat. "Could you drive us to the dean's office?"

Zane saw a frown cover Mathew's face before he climbed in behind the professor and sat in the back seat.

"Sure, my pleasure, is there a problem?" Mathew asked as he started the cart and drove slowly down the pathway.

"Just some questions young Zane has here about his final grades." Professor Davison said and Zane saw the man hold tight to the dash handle. When Mathew turned a corner quickly, he saw the professor squeezed the handle harder and gave a little squeal. His reactions confirmed to Zane that the man was terrified of either the cart's movements or Mathew's driving.

When they arrived, Zane wasn't shocked when Mathew followed them into the Head Dean's office. He knew from his prior conversations with Mathew that the man took a personal interest in Zane's education. But having him there increased Zane's uncertainty in the whole situation.

"Come in, come in." Head Dean Dickson said and walked around his desk to offer the three arrivals seats. "What can I do for you today?"

The pleasant smile on the Head Dean's face faltered when Zane asked about his grades.

"Sir, I need to know why my grades are not reflecting correctly." Zane stated, the ball of ice was back, but it had moved from his stomach to his throat. He found it difficult to even voice that simple of a question.

The Head Dean's face grew pale and his eyes quickly darted to where Mathew sat inches from Zane. The room grew silent as the many clock's continued to tick behind the Dean's desk.

"Ah, I think I can answer your question." It wasn't the Dean who answered, but Mathew. Turning, Zane saw the man frown once before he smiled again. "You see Zane, I told you about the donor." When Mathew paused, Zane nodded, not sure his voice worked anymore as he studied the man, somehow now fearing the answer. "Well, for the Academy to acquire the entire year's balance, all quarters must be passed."

Zane felt like the air in the room had vanished. The answer to his question was simple. The Academy was going to give him grades based on what the anonymous donor had stipulated, despite his own efforts.

"Zane, we want you to succeed, it isn't our intention for your grades to not reflect your hard work, however, in Professor Davison's coding class, well..." Mathew waved his hands and paused here as the professor sat forward.

"Actually, I might have a few suggestions regarding

our current dilemma." The professor stated with a smile on his round face.

ZANE COULDN'T BELIEVE his luck!

First, his final grade in Coding had been adjusted. Yes, it was now sitting at 82, but he had earned this score by himself, it hadn't been falsified on his behalf.

Professor Davison had asked Zane during yesterday's meeting all about his wheel rider. He had been interested in the coding and memory board Zane had used to tie the function of the wheel rider to the machines brain.

Zane explained that the circuits he had used were part of a Piper's memory board used for simple pipe variances.

"I re-wrote the main circuits so when the pressor board feels my feet lean left, the wheel lowers power on that side turning the board left." Zane explained to the professor who sat in awe at the rider's simplicity.

"But how did you bypass the memory board's main function?" The professor had asked and leaned closer as Zane continued with his explanation.

They spent a whole hour going over Zane's design, his circuit re-wiring and yes, 'coding'. Zane had never really thought of his wiring the rider, or the other inventions as 'coding'. So, when the professor wanted to grade him on the wheel rider, he was both shocked and pleased.

But the best news came after, when Professor Davison suggested he change his fifth period coding class with the second period class.

"I spend more time on circuits in this class than the one you are currently in. If we change with your government class, this will also put you in class with my best student. He can tutor you

in any of the number coding you currently struggle with." Professor Davison *said with a smile. "Also, I believe he's from your own hub."*

Zane's excitement was hard to contain, his grade was lower than previously, but now he was to attend the same class and be tutored by his best friend, Mitch. All because he stood up for what he had thought was right, the belief that you earn a grade yourself.

He had also learned an important fact during his meeting with the Dean and the Financial Advisor, Mathew. No matter what, Zane would never be expelled from the Academy, not while they wished to continue receiving the large funds from his unknown benefactor.

Excitement that night kept him awake, along with thoughts of who his benefactor could be. Thoughts floated in his mind, answers he couldn't proof, ideas that his unknown father maybe had paid for his schooling. Also, he pondered if the dead man from the Pipes had somehow left him the funds, but that was impossible as the man was dead and no one knew it was Zane who had witnessed the murder.

Each time he questioned who was supplying the funds, Mia's words would come back to him. *"This opportunity you cannot miss!"*

With excitement, he went to his first class the next day with a smile on his face. He had talked to Mitch the night before, who still insisted they pretend not to know each other, something they were getting really good at by now.

"You can't show any excitement." Mitch's *voice sounded a little higher across the line as they talked that night. "I mean it. Not a day goes by without one of the Professor's asking me about friends."*

"Maybe they are just concerned for you?" Zane had asked then shrugged his shoulders. "Either way, it was Professor Davison's idea. I doubt he's going to put us together because they suspect something."

"No, I guess not." Mitch's following hesitation had Zane thinking about the visit from the two men during his holiday.

"I think my benefactor is protecting me from the Primary." Zane stated and waited silently for Mitch's reply. When none came, he tried again. "Mitch, I think Waltson is my benefactor."

"But who is Waltson?" Mitch finally asked. "And why would he pay all that money to send you to the Academy?" Mitch's voice sounded doubtful, as Zane felt his own belief start to faulter.

"Too many questions and not enough answers." Zane finally said with a shake of his head. "Either way, we will get to talk to each other face to face tomorrow."

Zane was worried that his first period class would take forever. He knew the minutes ticked slower than normal and found his mind wondering while Professor Luthier talked about the printer's and their functions. He heard about the recyclers and their breakdown of materials back to their basic formula that the printers then used to re-form new items.

He didn't hear the professor talk at all about the fact that most Piper's couldn't afford to go to the printers, that they and even most of the Fixers used broken materials to build their own replacements. Most of the Piper and Fixer hub was rebuilt from discarded materials from the Primary hub, even the Academy's discards helped maintain the poorer hub's homes. As the professor continued to talk about the wonders of the printers and recyclers, Zane wondered why she didn't cover this important fact. He knew she didn't like him asking questions during her speeches, so jotted down a note to ask her after class.

Pipers and fixers use discarded materials?

He wrote on his tablet and looked up to see how much more time he had before the class was over.

Twenty minutes to go.

When the professor continued to talk of the wonders of how the world, they lived in, recycled everything, another question formed in Zane's mind as the dead man's image flashed into his mind's eyes.

What happens to a dead person's body?

This question was morbid, but he had never asked Mia. Maybe he should hold this question and research it himself? He moved to delete the question when he felt a small hand on his, turning he saw Breanna's eyes on his as she held his hand from hitting the delete button.

She blinked quickly and grabbed his tablet from the table. She started to type as the professor continued to give the lesson. When Breanna set the tablet on the desk in front of him, he saw her message.

Yes, the bodies are used for the sick. My father's heart beats in another's chest.

Her simple statement had questions popping in his mind. He knew nothing of the Primary, nor of Breanna, who he considered a friend, maybe something even more than a friend.

She sat quietly next to Zane every day and ate her meals with him and his friends, but they had never talked about personal things. Only school, lessons and daily events and assignments were spoken of, nothing personal.

Feeling suddenly that he didn't even know the pretty

girl he sat next to each day, he felt his face turn red. Grabbing his tablet, he typed a new message to her.

Sorry about your father. My mother is gone too.

He saw her nod as she typed a simple Thank you.

The rest of the lesson Zane's thoughts turned from the pretty Breanna to his other friends. Did he know anything about Rafe, Evan or even Miles? He knew Miles had grown up in this very hub, his parents were doctors or something like that. He knew Evan's was from the Fixer hub, and Rafe who was the oldest at sixteen was from the Primer hub.

He knew Evan was allergic to white veggie strips, and Miles hated green fruit substitute, despite them being processed. But beyond that, he only knew he counted them as friends. Setting a new goal for himself, he determined that he would know more about his friends, all of them, by the end of the day.

His goal was easier to obtain than he had thought. It appeared that after his private typed conversation with Breanna, she opened up to him as they walked out of base class.

"He died when I was young. But my mom has always been there for me." Breanna stated with a slight smile on her face. "She keeps busy with her work, but my grandmother keeps an eye on me when mom's away."

"My Mia, I mean grandmother raised me too." Zane said with a smile and found it was suddenly easier to talk to her because of what they had in common. He still felt shy and his palms still sweat a bit, but they had more in common than either of them had known.

When they finally parted ways and headed to their different second classes, Zane had a smile on his face. His excitement at being "introduced" to Mitch had him quickening his steps.

"Wait up!" Rafe said as he ran to join Zane. "Did you forget I have this class too?"

Zane had been pleased to find that Rafe also had the second period Coding class. This meant he now had three classes with the older boy. A boy he was quickly idolizing.

"Sorry, I'm just nervous about this class." Zane replied as they walked to the computer class.

"You'll like Mitch, I sit next to him in class." Rafe told him. "He's a bit quiet, but nice, young for his brains, if you know what I mean."

Zane said nothing, he was too shocked to realize his two friends had known each other this whole time.

"I'll warn you now, Weston and Manny also are in this class."

With Rafe's statement, Zane felt his stomach tighten with dread. But then he remembered his conversation with the Dean and Mathew. *He* couldn't be penalized or ejected from the Academy.

Feeling a smile slowly cross his lips, Zane followed Rafe into the classroom, determined to enjoy himself.

FRIENDS

Living without the inhibitions and restrictions or fears of being sent home delighted Zane. His smile felt wider, his steps lighter as he finished his school day.

He had a fleeting thought of skipping his schoolwork, but remembered he still needed to get through life after the Academy. This meant his schoolwork was more important to him, a boy with no father and no other avenues of work to fall back on once he was out of school.

If he could gain his vocation at the Academy, then he was in debt to whoever had presented this great gift to him. He now had the entire world before him, not just the pipes, which had already been denied to him.

With new determination he focused on his schoolwork until dinner. He still had his computer coding assignment to finish but he figured his time with Mitch would result in that being finished.

The tutor times had been set each evening after dinner at nineteen hundred. This hour with Mitch would eat into his relaxing time with his friends, but his excitement about getting to see Mitch overshadowed this. Mitch's warnings still rang in Zane's mind as he walked over to the building his friend was living in.

The building didn't look like a dorm building, it looked fancier in Zane's opinion. Glass panels lined the front of the tall structure and double wide doors with an automatic sensor silently swished open for him. The interior was even more impressive, tiled floors and white tall walls gave the entrance a feeling of vastness.

Knowing Mitch had a room on the main floor, Zane looked for the number 7 over the doors and found it on the third door to his left. Worried his voice could carry, he gently knocked on the door and waited.

Zane felt his smile widen when Mitch opened the door, but the grin fell away when he saw Mitch's pale face shake back and forth slightly, his eyes wide as he mouthed 'shh..'.

"Ah, you're late." He then said loudly and stepped back quickly. "We have been waiting."

'We?' Zane thought with confusion as he stepped forward and crossed into the room.

His confusion was short lived when he heard several voices coming from beyond the small entrance of Mitch's private room, or rooms as Zane quickly discovered.

Mitch, having won his time at the Academy, and due to his disability, had been provided the rooms normally reserved for professors. The entrance alcove was small, but it opened into a living space larger than the home Zane had grown up in.

A couch sat in a living space, windows which looked out at the green grass of a courtyard sat beyond. Lamps and a large hanging light caused the room to be cheerful. Two doors led off the main rooms, Zane saw one led to a private bathroom while the other had a bed visible beyond the door. A large metal table with six chairs stood before Zane, each chair full of students except one which he presumed had been Mitch's. Two girls and three boys looked up from the table and studied Zane with open curiosity.

"Sam, would you mind getting Zane a chair?" Mitch stated and while a tall boy with short brown hair rose to grab a chair from the bedroom, Mitch made introductions.

Thea and Whitney were the two girls, both about fifteen, Thea had blond hair while Whitney had long black hair. Zane recognized both girls from his class while the three boys he didn't recognize. Brian who was a short boy which Zane struggled to guess his age age, but speculated it was about Jack's age around sixteen. Jack the second boy had braces on his teeth and smiled as Sam the third boy brough Zane a chair.

"We have another thirty minutes to discuss our Government assignment, if you want you can join in and then after everyone leaves, I will have time to go over coding with you." Mitch explained as he leaned his crutch against the wall after sitting down.

Zane hadn't brought his Government class assignment, so he sat quietly as the group continued to discuss their day's assignment. After listening for a minute, Zane quickly grabbed his tablet and pulled up his already finished assignment for that class.

He discovered several of the key elements of his paper had been completed wrong. Making quick notes, he realized he would have to complete several adjustments when he got back to his dorm that night.

When the half hour was up, three of the students left. Thea the blond girl and the short boy Brian remained behind.

"Now, on to coding." Mitch said with a shake of his head. Brian here has the same struggles you do Zane. Thea knows the number's aspect of coding but struggles with the layout." Mitch continued and quickly dove into the day's lessons that Professor Davison had provided them.

Zane soon found his concept of that day's coding lessons a little easier to follow, but his excitement over seeing Mitch had waned a little. He worried that he wouldn't have any alone time with his friend.

Mitch's explanation of the professor's lessons gave Zane a new admiration for his friend. He now had a better understanding how he had easily won the lottery granting him access to the Academy at such a young age. An hour after the session started resulted in Zane's completed assignment and firmer grasp of Professor Davison's lesson's concepts.

Thea was the first to leave and when Brian rose to leave, Zane felt hopeful he and Mitch would finally have some time alone.

"You can't stay long." Mitch warned after he shut the door behind Brian. "They are always watching."

Zane felt deflated but Mitch quickly reminded him they still had the TWT's that would allow them to talk privately.

With his assignment finished, Zane nodded and placed a hand on Mitch's right shoulder.

"It is good to see you again." Zane explained with a smile. "And I think with your help, my grades will improve in Coding."

Mitch's lopsided smile flashed at him before he ducked his head. "You never needed my help; your inventions were always coded well."

"Yes, well I am learning there is a difference between doing and learning." Zane explained and picked up his tablet to leave.

"Talk to you later?" Mitch asked.

"Of course." Zane said before he left, somehow just being around Mitch had lightened his mood.

Returning to his dorm room, he reminded himself that he still had a mission, his promise to learn about his Dorm mates. Rafe and Miles were missing when he returned so he smiled at Evan as he walked in. Evan was laying across his bunk, a book in his hands but a smile on his face when he saw Zane.

"Hey Even." Zane stated as he walked into Evan's cube.

"Hey, what are you doing?" Evan asked and put the book down.

"Just finished getting tutored." Zane explained with a smile and sat down in the desk's chair. "Evan, you're from the fixer hub, right?"

"Yeah." Evan sat up and looked at Zane, confusion and speculation on his face. "Why?"

Shrugging his shoulders, Zane settled into the chair more comfortably. "Never been there, what's it like?"

Evan smiled with the question and quickly explained that he was an only child. He and his family lived in a what he called a town house building in the Fixer hub. It appeared they were fortunate and his parents held a high level in their hub because when Evan's dad had finished training him, they decided to send him to the Academy so Evan could gain a higher level also.

"Mom and Dad are both fixers, Mom works for the Advisor which pays more credits than dad gets, but he likes working with the softer metals. He really favors wood, but it's scarce in the fixer hub." Evan explained with a smile.

"Did you have lots of friends there?" Zane asked as he tried to image a life with both parents.

"Yeah, and some family too. Dad's got a cousin and he and his family live in the same building." Evan replied with a shrug. "But with the limitations, they're the only family besides my Mom's parents. How about you?"

"Limitations?" Zane asked with confusion. "What limitations?"

"You know." Evan responded with a smile that faltered when Zane continued to stare at him. "The restriction on the family size. Course I know one boy whose parents were approved to have a second child which is when he got stuck with a bratty little sister."

Completely confused now, Zane leaned forward as he studied his friend. "Evan, what are you talking about?"

Sitting up fully now, Evan studied Zane with his dark eyes. "Are you saying the Piper's don't have a limit on how many kids they can have?"

"Why would there be a limit?" Zane asked with a shake of his head. "The more kids, the more credits, and the more workers who can go down in the pipes." Zane stated and a thought passed in his mind that maybe Evan was trying to play a joke on him.

"No limit?" Evan asked and quickly stood from his

bed. When he rushed out of the room, Zane had a fleeting thought that maybe the boy wasn't joking.

"Here, come here." Evan's voice sounded as he dragged Tyler their Dorm Advisor into the room. "Tyler, how many kids are the fixer's allowed to have?" The question was almost shouted at the advisor, who stood in the doorway looking entirely confused.

"What? What are you talking about?" Tyler asked and turned to look at Zane. "You know if you want more than one, you have to get a permit from the Primary Administrator."

"See!" Evan exclaimed and pointed at Tyler. "The Pipers don't have any restrictions!"

When Tyler laughed, Zane felt his world grow muddled. What he knew about his world, up to now, seemed to be a lot less than before.

"How does your hub support an unlimited growth?" Tyler asked Zane as he continued to stand there with his mouth open in astonishment.

"What? Oh, well not many live to my Grandmother's age." Zane finally answered. "Of course, each year we lose about fifty in the pipes. There's always a blown pressure accident, or sometimes kids wander from their father's side and get lost or fall down an exposed shaft." When Zane shrugged his shoulders at the inevitability of tragic and dangers of the Pipes the two boys gapped at him with shock on their face.

"You're telling us that kids go down into the pipes and die?" Evan asked shocked. "Actually die?"

"Well, if there's an accident, then yeah." Zane explained. "That's why most families have several kids."

"He said they get more credits for more kids. Didn't you?" Evan asked Zane.

Zane felt his knowledge of ECHO grow dim; he found himself explaining to his Dorm mates about life in the Pipes. At one-point Rafe and Miles walked in and then they quickly asked their questions about life in the Pipes.

It appeared that Fixers, Primary's and even Recyclers and Printers all had a limit on having children. They also didn't get credits per children, which shocked Zane until he found out that each worker in these hubs earned more a day than most Piper's did in a week.

"How can the government afford to pay all of that?" Zane asked in amazement.

"Well, each earns their own way." Rafe said with confusion. "I mean our families work."

"But how?" Zane asked. In his mind the Pipers were hard workers, they rode the rail carts down into the pipes each morning and returned ten hours later, dirty and exhausted. And if there was an accident, then they would also return with the dead.

"There is always need for the fixers." Evan explained with a shake of his dark head.

"And doctors and other medical techs are in high demand." Miles spoke up.

"What about the Primer hub?" Zane asked as eyes turned to Rafe.

"Well," Rafe looked stunned for a minute as he thought. "You've got the government officials, credit financiers, the banks and other clerical jobs."

Shaking his head, Zane found it hard to believe that

someone sitting at a desk all day would earn more credits than those down in the pipes. The pipes that kept ECHO alive.

"Zane, what would happen if the pipes weren't worked?" Mile's quiet question had four pair of eyes looking at him with concern.

Taking a deep breath, Zane thought of his secretive times in the pipes. Of how he had snuck into the vast tunnels each night. How sometimes he had found valves needing to be adjusted, pressure release switches that required imitate modifications.

Then he thought of the times the warning bells would ring indicating an accident had happened. How each family member who didn't travel down into the pipes would then run out of their huts and homes. Women with fear on their faces, young children confused by the chaos.

Zane knew that if the men and women no longer went down into the pipes, than ECHO would fall apart on itself, maybe in a vast explosion of gas, air and water.

Finally shaking his head, they all must have seen his answer in his eyes. Miles quickly stood and started to pace the distance between the four bunks while Rafe ran a hand through his hair several times and cussed.

"But they won't stop!" Tyler insisted and turned to look at Evan. "Why would they?"

"Tyler, why do fixers work?" Evan asked his fellow fixer.

"They work for credits." Tyler said and a small smile formed on his lips. "Of course, the Pipers will continue to work, for credits."

"But how is it they don't know how much the other hubs earn?" Rafe asked with a shake of his head. "You make it sound like they continued to work for mere credits compared to what other's earn."

"I don't think they know." Zane replied with a shake of his head.

"Then your only here because of the donation?" Mile's question had everyone's eyes returning to him.

"Yes, I was sent here because of the donor who funded my full education, and before you ask, I still don't know who is paying my way." Zane said with a shake of his head. "I only know that the Academy gets a large amount for each level I complete."

"Why you?" Evan's question wasn't something new to Zane. He had asked that very question himself since he had arrived at the school.

"I don't know that either. I have no immediate family other than Mia; I don't even know my father which is why I hold the last name of Noman." Zane explained and felt the old shame return from not knowing his own father's name.

Zane missed his secret meeting time with Mitch that night. Instead he and the other boys sat awake most of the night asking each other about themselves and their hubs to see if there were any more differences.

At one-point Miles had pulled out his tablet and started researching about the hubs only to be disappointed in what little the E-libraries had. A general description was given, but the lives and livelihood of the hubs were missing.

Each boy had a long list of questions they wanted to aske before they finally called it a night. Questions they vowed they would ask their professors the next day.

The breakfast meal was quickly eaten, each boy tired

from the lack of sleep, but anxious to get to Base class and ask Professor Luthier some of their questions. They had all agreed that Rafe should start, but by his second question, Professor Luthier had shut down all of Rafe's questions with a wave of her thin hand.

"These types of questions should be submitted in writing to the Administration department. They will answer any further queries you have." She then continued with her lessons as if Rafe hadn't asked important life altering questions.

Their frustration increased when each boy proceeded to ask their own questions to each professor during their separate classes. Each time they were provided with the same answers. Submit your questions in writing, and then lessons would continue as if there had been no interruption at all.

That night, before Zane had picked up his wheel rider to head to his tutor lessons, they had all decided that Zane should be the one to submit the questions.

"Look, we know you can't be expelled. If the professors won't answer these questions, it may mean they don't want students asking them. If a student could get into trouble by asking, then maybe it should be you asking?" Rafe suggested.

"I can type them up." Miles suggested quickly. "Since you have to go to your lessons. That might help." Miles usually bored expression was grim instead, his brown eyes sober as a frown formed on his lips.

Giving him a nod, Zane then headed over to Mitch's. He knew their large number of questions could possibly change the way the hubs live. But he and his friends all agreed, they wanted answers.

Mitch and the other students were busy when he arrived. Since he remembered bringing his Government class assignment, he sat down and immediately jumped into the discussion.

When the topic turned to Coding, Whitney, Jake and Sam stood to leave. Coding, under Mitch's guidance, seemed more understandable to Zane. It seemed that Professor Davison's monotone droning about numbers were starting to make sense to Zane while he was in the class.

Each lesson provided little insights for him and Zane keep thinking of ways he could use the knowledge to make adjustments to his Rider. If he connected two circuits to the sensor pads, he could have the wheel rider able to make faster turns or stopping quicker.

When the study group was over and the others had left, Mitch quickly asked about Zane missing the prior night's meeting time.

"Sorry, I'll tell you tonight. It's important and you should know about it. But not know." Zane urged and after putting a hand on Mitch's shoulder gave him a frown. "It changes our world." With this statement he nodded once and then quickly left.

TRUTHS

Miles had finished typing up the questions by the time Zane returned to the dorm room that night. As they all watched he email the document to the Administration department. For good measure, Zane also sent a copy to the Head Dean and Mathew too. After sending the questions, he quickly grabbed his TWT and slipped into the bathroom to talk privately to Mitch.

"You didn't send it, did you?" Mitch's voice sounded scared not shocked, when Zane had explained about his discoveries.

"Of course, I just sent it." Zane replied, confused by Mitch's lack of shock.

"Zane, you have to delete it! You shouldn't have sent it!" Mitch's concerned voice confused him further.

"Why not?"

"Zane, don't you think the Primary already knows all of this? Why do you think the segregation between our hub and the others has gone on for so long?" Now Mile's voice sounded like he was frustrated. "You should have talked to me first!"

"Why?" Zane quickly asked, hurt and worried at the same time.

"Zane, don't you understand, our government has encouraged the separation of the Pipers from the other hubs. There is a reason why our hub can't afford to send their kids to the Academy, there's also a reason why we never had, nor heard of the child restrictions."

"We figured that out, it's the dangers." Zane said smugly.

"That and other reasons." Mitch said quickly. "Don't you see, if other hubs found out the Piper's didn't have a restriction, then they would move there, but they couldn't, not with the dangers. If the Piper's found out their dangerous lives were worth less than the others, they would revolt against doing the work. Important work. Then where would this world be? Dead, that's where." Mitch's now angry tone shocked Zane.

"What are you saying? I thought you would be outraged to learn that your families dangerous job earned less than some wimpy person sitting behind a desk in the Primary hub?"

"Of course, I was shocked!" Mitch's words started to sink in as Zane listened to his friend. "Why should my family's lives be put in danger each day, yet the small credit earned was a constant struggle for us. How could we live in such a poor state when we were paying so much with our very lives?" Mitch explained. "But do you think that my uneducated father or mother could change this? No, even if all the Pipers stand together and say no more, all this will accomplish is the sudden death of this world and all who live in it." There was a long pause before Mitch continued, this time his young voice sounded tired. "Zane, the way ECHO is run can only be changed by those who run it."

"You mean the Primary." Zane stated and felt the truth of Mitch's words sink in.

"Yes." Came the single reply.

"Mitch, can it really cause harm asking?" Zane feared his friend's answer.

"For you? No. But you must urge your friends to refrain from asking these questions or even spreading the hint of difference. For now." Mitch replied.

Zane knew his friend was correct. After signing off and getting ready for bed, he asked Tyler and the others to gather for a quick meeting. He tried to explain the dangers and urged them to remain quiet, for now. All except Rafe agreed.

"Look, I don't see any harm in asking, but for now I will hold my tongue." He finally stated. "But living in the main hub, I am offended by my government's treatment of those who keep this very world alive."

"I understand." Zane agreed with a nod of his head which was pounding by the time the discussion was finished.

That night Zane found his sleep was fitful. He dreamed of the tunnels filled with pipes, something that was so familiar to him, but in his dark dreams the pipes seemed to be a forest of the unknown. Twists and turned blocked his way forward, a way he didn't seem to know. When the pipes turned into people, the transition seemed normal to his sleeping mind.

There at a rather dangerous corner was Weston and

his friends, they hissed and threatened to blow up in Zane's face before he rushed pass them. Then there were professors blocking his path. Each shaking their fingers and heads at him as he tried to rush past.

Breanna and his dorm friends stood there too, but each one kept trying to direct him down another darkened path. Even in his sleeping state he knew what lay at the end of his dreaming journey.

When the dead man stood blocking his path, Zane tried look away. The blood oozed out of the massive hole in his chest as the man's eyes looked back at him.

"So many tunnels, how is it you knew where to find me?" The man accused. "Did you do this to me?"

"No!" Zane tried to back up but found the walls had closed him in, locking him in with the dead.

"You did nothing to help me!" The man accused. "Nothing!"

When Zane awoke the next morning, sweat had dried and made his night clothing stick to his arms and chest. A sour taste was in his mouth and he rushed to the bathroom where he got sick.

"We should call the nurse!" Came a voice from behind him as he stood from his bent position near the toilet.

"Are you ill?" Rafe asked as he and Miles eyed Zane from the bathroom doorway.

"Just..." Zane didn't want to tell them about the dream so thought up a lie, but nothing came to his foggy mind. "Just threw up is all."

He moved to the sink and brushed his teeth while his two friends eyed him. Miles moved over and studied him with doubt on his face.

"Could be something you ate." Miles supplied and automatically reached up to feel Zane's forehead.

"Get off! What are you doing?" Zane asked as he tried to step away.

"He's clammy, hot too." Miles said with a shake of his head. "Go get Tyler."

"I don't need Tyler!" Zane said but the sound of his whiny voice concerned him.

"Back to your bunk." Rafe ordered with a shake of his head. "We don't want whatever you got." The older boy said and pointed a long finger at Zane. "Now."

"I have classes." Zane heard the high-pitched whine and tried to cringe but couldn't find enough energy to argue further.

"Now, or I'll have to carry your unconscious bones to bed myself." Rafe ordered again with a frown on his face.

Knowing his friends were right, Zane shuffled back to his bed. Even before he was finished laying down, Miles was back with Tyler.

"I have the nurse on the way." Tyler explained as Zane closed his eyes. "Are you three feeling fine?"

"No issues here, just the little guy." Zane heard Rafe say as he drifted back to sleep.

When he woke again there was an older lady standing over his bed. She had a frown on her wrinkled face as Zane tried to sit up.

"Stay still." She urged and using a bony hand, pushed Zane's head back on his pillow. "Probably just too much food and not enough sleep. You four, no excuses, head to class. I will take care of him."

Zane had his temperature taken and two pills shoved down his burning throat. Then he was told to sleep again, something he didn't argue with, and was asleep long before the nurse left his dorm.

Mia's face swam into his vision when he finally awoke again. Thinking he was back home, he smiled and tried to jump from his bed to do his chores before he remembered he wasn't in his home hub, but at school.

"Stay still." Mia urged and Zane saw concern filled her face. "You gave us all a good scare."

"Mia? What are you doing here?" Zane asked and felt that each word ripped a hole in his burning throat and then felt a very empty feeling in his stomach.

"Well, I had to come and get you back on your feet, now didn't I?" Mia asked and shook her head.

"You came?" Again, searing pain ripped along his throat.

"Of course." This time, Mia stood and walked over to a large chair next to the bed.

Seeing the room, Zane realized he wasn't in his dorm anymore. The room was completely white, a thin curtain encircled his bed and the chair that Mia sat down in.

"Where?" He tried to clear his throat but since it caused more pain, stopped there.

"Well, turns out you needed your appendix out." Mia said with a shake of her head. "Gave me a scare, your fever was too high, and the doctor was worried about that as well." Mia shook her head and smiled. "Your friend Miles, it was his mother who did your surgery." Mia told him. "All of your friends have been by today. Even a pretty little quiet girl." Mia gave him a sly smile. "I think she said her name was Breanna."

"Here?" Zane asked and tried to pull the covers higher on his chest and felt an odd little tug from his stomach.

Reaching down he felt a little pain when his fingers brushed the incisions but when he removed his hand, the odd feeling went away.

Mia gave a laugh and leaned back in the chair. "Oh, I know you'll be okey if you can still blush."

Zane soon was being given a large dish of cool flavored ice. The burning in his throat lessened and he took comfort knowing Mia was staying in the large chair next to him which could be turned into a sleeping bed.

"You should be back at school in another day, but that fever scared us." Doctor Sanderson had told him that night on her rounds. "Miles has been by twice today; I've seen more of him since you have been here than I usually do." She was a pretty brunette, her doctor's uniform was crisp and clean, but she had kind eyes that reminded Zane of her son's.

That night in the hospital, Zane slept fitfully. He wasn't sure if it was the fever or the drugs that they gave him, but his usually active dreams seemed to extraordinary. His dreams had always been imaginative, wild rides of his imagination and subconscious that always gave him a laugh after he awoke.

That night he dreamt of the Pipes, but in his dream the tunnels were all painted white. Clean shinny pipes lined the walls and ceiling and hundreds of people walked about, each with wheel riders.

When he tried to focus on a passing person, he saw it was Professor Luthier, her long skinny form danced about him and she tried to tell him the Pipes were not important.

"It's the admins that run this world." She said and then zipped away.

She was quickly replaced by another professor on a rider who tried to tell Zane the same thing.

Waking, he was so disorientated it took him a while to notice that Mia was no longer sleeping in the odd bed next to him. He tried to sit up and took courage when the pain in his side didn't hurt as bad as the day before.

"You should take it easy young fellow." Came a male voice from the doorway.

Quickly turning his head, he saw a familiar looking gray haired gentleman standing, his hand on a walker and a bandage on his arm. It took a second for Zane to remember the man's name.

"Adam?" Zane asked as he settled back against his pillow.

"Ah, you remember me." Adam said, a smile crossed his face as he took a small step inside Zane's room. "I didn't know if you would."

Adam wasn't wearing his chest plate with the blue lights today, but neither was Zane. Seeing the bandage on Adam's arm, Zane squinted and pointed a finger at it.

"What did you do?" He asked and saw Adam's smile widen.

"Ah, nothing quite as exciting as getting my appendix out, just a little blood drawn was all. But due to my age, they wanted to make sure I was well looked after." Adam explained and took another small step into the room. "And you, are you well after your surgery?"

Nodding, Zane realized that despite the odd dreams, the night's sleep had done him good. "Yeah, they say I might get to go back to school today."

Adam took a large breath and nodded. He was quiet for a moment as he continued to study Zane.

"Will you get to go back to the Pipes?" Zane finally asked.

"Ah, yes, I will be heading home today." Adam stated and nodded his head once more. "Are you enjoying your education?"

It was Zane's turn to nod.

"Well then, I think I had better return to my room before the nurse worries where I am." Adam said as he shuffled out the door. He turned back to Zane before he disappeared. "I am glad you are feeling better. Take care of yourself." He said and then disappeared down the hallway.

Zane was discharged later that afternoon with strict instructions to take it easy. This meant no heavy lifting, long walks, or too much excitement. He was also instructed to drink lots of fluids and eat healthy meals.

When Mia helped him into his dorm, he saw her eyes grow wide, much like his had the first time he had seen the dorm. He showed her his bunk and private closet space including the desk and books. He then introduced her to his friends, but since she had already meet them during his stay in the hospital, she just smiled.

"I will make sure he follows my mother's instructions." Miles stated and turned pink when Mia thanked him.

"Well, I better get going, the cart will be here soon to return me home." Mia said with a shake of her head.

"Mia." Zane said as he walked her down to the street. "How much was the operation?" Fear over their small pile of credits had him asking. He worried that she would be too busy filling orders in an attempt to pay for his procedure. This fear had him worried for her.

"Nothing, when I asked, I was informed it had been paid for by your donor." Mia said and tried to fix his school uniform's stiff collar. "We owe this person, you must study hard now and please, take care of yourself."

Zane had missed three days of school while he recovered. These three days meant that he spent the following eight days trying to catch up on his schoolwork.

His time with Mitch wasn't spent talking but instead he tried to catch up on several assignments. Even his free time wasn't free. Twice he had worked through mealtimes, luckily Miles had been eager to bring back something for him to eat.

Each night he fell into his bed, exhausted, too tired to do much other than close his eyes. When he did find a minute to think, his mind was usually full of questions about his unknown donor or the dead man. But he never came up with any answers, so he returned his focus to his work.

Twice Weston and his friends tried to make trouble for him. The first was the second day he was back from his surgery. They had followed Zane and Miles from the electronics class, but luckily Rafe and Evan had been nearby hoping to walk them to lunch.

Rafe thought the three bullies had tried to corner Zane knowing he might still be weak. This thought enraged Miles who had taken it as a personal mission to see that Zane recovered fully.

The second attempt was right before Base class. Breanna had been saving Zane a seat, but Weston had tried to sit there instead. He had then started to tease Breanna who quickly stood and walked to the front of the class and sat in one of the empty seats nearest to where the professor sat.

When Zane had sat next to her, he had been pelted with wads of paper each time the professor's back was turned. When a rather large clump hit him right behind his left ear he stood quickly and yelled at Weston who still had his arm pulled back to throw another ball at him.

"Stop it!" Zane yelled to everyone's shock.

Professor Luthier had not been amused, but to the entire class's shock, she had asked him quietly to please sit back down. Of course, Zane knew why he hadn't gotten into trouble, his unknown donor ensured that he wouldn't get into trouble, but that was his secret. Only he and his three dormmates knew this.

With a rather large smile aimed over his shoulder towards Weston, Zane took pleasure when no more paper wads hit him the rest of the class.

"Are you going?" Breanna's words interrupted Zane's thoughts one day during lunch. He had been thinking about a rather difficult coding program he wanted to try using on his wheel rider that he had learned in yesterday's class and appeared to have missed the conversation.

"What?" Zane asked and turned to study her.

"Zane!" Her exasperated tone she sometimes used towards him always made him smile. It usually meant she thought he was teasing her. "The new year's party. Are you going?"

"What party?" Zane hadn't heard of any parties during his whole time at the Academy. In fact, up to now he didn't know if the school allowed gatherings, other than academic ones.

"Well, it's not really a party as much as a get-together."

Breanna explained as she turned her focus back to her plate of veggie hash. "Delany's aunt lives here, she's a rather young medical assistant, only ten years older than Delany. I guess it took her mom's parents that long to get a second child certificate. Anyway, she invited Delany over to celebrate the new year and said she could invite a few friends. I thought that it would be fun if you and your friends would come and she said it would be fine. Delany also has her dorm friends coming too."

"Sounds like fun." Zane said with a smile. His excitement over the new year's had just increased. Usually the Academy only celebrated the annual holiday by not having classes on the first day of the new year. Zane had been told that was because students tended to stay up to see the clocks turn over, but he had heard the professors also had a hard time getting to class the next day.

"Where and when?" Zane asked with a smile.

THE PARTY

Evan was excited about the party, he informed Zane that he and his parents usually stayed up for the new year, but this would be his first non-parent party.

"Mom usually makes her homemade stew, wheat noodles and all." Evan told them.

"We know, you've only told us about ten times." Miles sounded bored, but Zane had seen the boy check the mirror several times while he was getting ready.

They had all changed out of their school uniforms and Zane thought Rafe's clothing was odd. The older boy's black pants matched his shirt, which had a short collar with a line of gold running through it. But it was Rafe's shoes that Zane thought were amazing. High top imitation leather black shoes, white soles and gold buckles held Zane's interest since Rafe had pulled them out of his closet. He studied them with a little envy, then goggled when Rafe pulled out a matching over shirt.

"It's called a jacket." Rafe said when he noticed Zane's

eyes on the garment. "Not really needed with the temperature mitigation in the hubs, but all the kids are wearing them at home." Rafe explained with a shrug of his broad shoulders.

"Mia has a shawl." Zane replied with a shrug. "She uses it when she works, she says sitting at the sewing machine all day makes her 'feel the air'." Zane said and returned Rafe's shrug with one of his own.

"A while back," Evan said with a grin, "all the Fixer kids tried to wear these large pants with lots of pockets." The smile on Evan's face had Zane grinning too. "Said it was cool to have the pockets filled to the brim with stuff. Me? I thought it made everyone look fat."

"I think I'll leave the jacket here." Rafe murmured and took the jacket off.

"No, it looks good on you." Evan said, I mean it's not jumbo pockets, but it goes with those killer shoes."

"Hay Z!" Miles turned to study him, a bored look on his face, but once again his eyes betrayed excitement. "Are you going to take the Z-rider?"

The guys had taken to calling Zane, by Z. It was a nickname Zane rather liked, he felt it made him sound cool. The rider had also become a big hit with his bunkmates and Evan was the first to suggest they call it the Z-rider, he was enthralled with it. Each day one of them would borrow his invention to run to a class, or sometimes just cruise around the hub. Zane and Miles had started to build circuit boards for three more riders, one for each of his friends. However, the complete construction of the riders had been delayed as there were no spare tires laying around the Academy hub.

"Nah, I think I'll just walk with you guys." Zane said and eyed his closet where he kept the rider.

"He just wants to be able to walk Breanna back to her dorm after the party." Evan teased.

Zane felt his face heat up and knew his ears were turning red again. Ducking his head, he bent and pretended to tie his shoe as his friends all laughed at his embarrassment.

"Zap off." Rafe hissed after a moment and helped Zane back to his feet. "They're just jealous."

Zane took a deep breath and nodded, then once again shrugged his shoulders. "I don't mind."

"That's the ticket." Rafe urged and slung his arm around Zane's shoulder. "Come on, our girls are waiting."

Somehow Rafe always made Zane feel better about himself. The older boy not only protected Zane physically, but emotionally too. If Zane had an older brother, he wanted him to be just like Rafe.

The four friends walked over to the girl's dorm, a shiny glass building that was three blocks down and two over. Breanna had her hair up and little curls hung down by her pretty face. The orange dress reminded Zane that she was from the main hub, it sparkled and looked more expensive than anything he had ever seen before. Breanna's friend Delany wore long black pants with a little silky top and wore a short jacket over it which covered her arms.

Rafe's girlfriend Asher was there too. The redhead had on a purple dress. It didn't have any of Breanna's sequins, a word he was told by Breanna when he asked about the shiny orbs, but it too looked expensive.

Before he had left their dorm, Zane had felt good

about his new pants from Mia, but now he was reminded of the differences between the hubs once more. Despite his odd feelings, his friends talked and laughed with each other on the way to the party. After about three blocks, Zane shook the negative feelings away and started to enjoy his friend's company once more.

Rafe and Ash were holding hands, something Evan and Miles were currently snickering at. The teasing didn't seem to bother the older boy or his girl, but it sent heat creeping into Zane's ears once more.

Would Breanna expect him to hold her hand?

Just the thought of this had his steps faltering as they neared Delany's aunt's home.

"Francine has lived here two years." Delany was telling them as they approached the high building's front entrance.

Double wide glass doors with shiny brass trimming open into a wide foyer. The tile floors mirrored some of the same stones that could be found inside several school buildings, but the feeling was different. Large brass vases lined the walls and bright paintings hung above each one. Each painting held colors and a feeling of movement that Zane had never seen before.

Each picture had shown what Zane didn't know, what no one alive in ECHO had ever know. In several pictures he saw vast green blankets rolled up to meet deep blue. White puffs floated in the blue, and a far-off purple triangle or two could be seen in the distance.

When they stepped into the elevator, Zane's eyes were still on the paintings. He felt a tightness in his throat as the doors blocked the beautiful image from him. Feeling highly uncomfortable at this, he blinked quickly and cleared his throat.

When he felt Breanna's small hand on his arm, he looked down and saw her smile.

"I know." She whispered and then quickly removed her hand.

Did she? Did she understand that he had never, ever seen anything so emotionally beautiful before?

"What?" Zane asked her quietly while the others continued to talk around them.

"They are landscapes." Breanna explained and studied him once more. "Pictures of the outside world, or what we had once lived in."

Her words and meaning buzzed around inside his head as the exited the elevator. The paintings were just hung in the lobby, did these people pass them every day without knowing how precious they were? Had anyone from his hub seen anything like it? It took Zane a while to shake the feelings the pictures had induced deep in him.

Francine's apartment was smaller than the dorm the four boys lived in. But it had an open floorplan with the eating area and vast windows facing out at the wall of the hub.

Soft curtains and two deep red couches made the space comfortable. Francine was only ten years older than Delany, but she had already finished the Academy's fifth level with honors and been chosen to be a doctor's apprentice two months before she had started her sixth level classes. That was three years ago, and Francine was now a rising assistant.

Delany's introduction to her aunt showed Zane the two girls were more sisters than aunt and niece. Francine had two more friends show up, both girls who were also doctor's assistances, a tall skinny blond named Rebecca and a noticeably short dark girl named Yvette.

The group talked about the Academy, Rebecca liked to talk about the professors and people they used to know while Yvette talked about their jobs and the lessons or work itself.

Zane realized before the meal was served that Breanna kept close to him. He wasn't sure if she was shy around these people, but he took comfort in her presence. Since his discovery of her father's death, he had found it easier to talk to her.

At one point the conversation had turned to his Z-rider. He wasn't sure who brought up the rider, but was sure it was Evan.

"I sure could use something like that." Rebecca said with a little frown. "I live six blocks from work and some-times I'm so tired at the end of my shift that walking home seems to take forever."

"How many credits are these Z-riders?" Francine asked, her eyes on Evan.

"Z built it." Evan said with a smile. "But I'm sure we can talk him into a reasonable price."

BEFORE THE END of the party, Zane found himself with three orders for new Z-riders. Each girl was willing to pay twenty-five credits, this high amount usually took Mia sixteen days to earn by selling clothes.

Evan urged the girls to give Zane a deposit of half before he would start on the riders. The rest of the credits would be collected upon delivery and came with a private lesson by one of the boys to ensure they would know how to operate the riders.

"Are they hard to ride?" Rebecca asked, concern on her face.

"Not at all, we just want to give you your credit's worth, and lessons are included." Evan, the natural seller of the group, said with a wink and smile.

The remaining conversation through dinner was about the riders. Evan's excitement over the rider kept the mood high even through desert.

After the meal was consumed, Francine handed out small poppers, a paper roll that emitted a loud pop when you opened them to gain the prize hidden within. Breanna had to help Zane with his, having never seen one, he was shocked to see a silver ring inside. Such an expensive gift inside a package confused him until Breanna whispered that the rings were a normal New Year's gift.

The girls received pretty hair barrettes; Breanna's was a pretty purple that she immediately put in her hair. Zane, still holding his ring, smiled and slipped it on his middle finger with a shrug of his shoulders.

The walk back to their dorm that night, or the next morning, was filled with laughter and talks of the mass production of the Z-riders. Evan talked about filing a certificate with the fixer board so they could legally sell the riders.

"It will all be in your name so you will need to go with me." Evan's words had Zane smiling.

"I've never been to the Fixer hub." He replied.

"You'll love it!" Evan said and slapped Zane on his back. "Tomorrow we'll go. You can meet my parents!"

"Z, what do you need to finish our riders?" Rafe's

question had Zane thinking about the four unfinished boards.

"I need wheels, and if I have three more to build, I will need more circuits." He replied.

"How about the battery packs?" Miles reminded him.

"Sounds like we may need to go to the Printers." Rafe commented.

"Actually, we might find everything we need at the Recyclers." Miles provided with a shake of his shoulders referring to the other half of the Printer hub where all used, broken or unwanted items were taken to be broken down into their natural elements so the printers could use them in creating new products.

The farewell to the girls was quick that night, they dropped each off at their dorm, Rafe gave Ash a quick kiss. The smooch was something the other boys teased him about all the way back to their dorm.

Before bed that night, all four boys went over the status of the riders. Evan urged Zane to draw a diagram of the circuit board and the rider's themselves.

"The committee will need to see this before they will allow you to sell them." Evan explained after they awoke early.

Having the next day off from schoolwork, all four of the boys spent the morning working on the Z-riders. Rafe suggested they split their load by having him and Miles running the errand over to the recyclers.

"Miles and I can pick up the items needed for the new riders, along with the wheels while you two go and file for the certificate." Rafe explained.

After finishing the shopping list, Zane reminded Rafe about the size of the wheels needed for the riders and then they were off. Rafe and Miles heading towards the Printer hub to pick up used parts while he and Evan took a cart and headed towards the Fixer hub.

Zane's excitement over seeing a new hub kept him on the edge of the E-cart's seat. When they moved beyond the main hub and down the long tunnel leading to the Fixer hub, he leaned forward.

Evan had been talking the entire drive. He told Zane of the hub's qualities, how each home was filled with inventions. Some so old that the inhabitance no longer knew how to fix them.

"We never throw anything away if it has working parts." Evan explained and Zane swore he heard pride in the boy's voice. "My Grandma has a hand tool from before ECHO was finished."

This statement distracted Zane until they came out of the dark tunnel and entered the Fixer hub.

In Zane's hub was filled with odd metal sheds and homes, each building was stacked near or sometimes on top of each other. Cold grey metal slabs made up the homes in the Piper hub giving it a unification look of misery.

Here, Zane found bright colors that reminded him of the pretty paintings in the entrance of Francine's lobby. Red, yellow, blue and orange homes filled Zane's vision. The homes were close, some stacked upon one another, but each held their own personality.

Bright white windows and doors reflected the hub's overhead lights. Here and there a home held a large contraption sitting on its roof. Levers and wheels perched high as if waiting to spring into action at any moment.

Near the center of the hub Zane saw taller buildings

much like any other hub. But these buildings held odd metal tubes that twisted around the outside.

"Slides." Evan said with a smile. "Built long ago. It's a rather fun invention of a man named Brian Evanson. I'm named after him." The pride was in Evan's voice again as he continued to drive down the lane towards the far side of the hub.

They passed several large buildings, each with inventions in various stages of disrepair, some looked finished while other's looked like they had been stripped of all working parts, only skeletons of their former selves.

"There, see that!" Evan urged as they rounded a corner, and a new street of odd inventions came into view. "That's my dad's invention."

The invention in question was a large metal beast. It loomed two stories above the house it sat in front of. Since Zane didn't know what he was looking at, he nodded and remained quiet.

"It helps clear the streets." Evan explained with a smile. Dad has to use it twice a week, so the streets stay clear." As they neared the home, Zane saw large claws which sat under the tall machine and he tried not to shiver. "The council sends out a warning first, then the next day dad drives the Leviathan out to clear the roads."

"Evan!" The high shriek came from the doorway of the home they had stopped in front of. A slender grey-haired woman came running down the orange steps and threw herself at his friend.

"Mom!" Evan said and lifting the woman off her feet, gave her a quick spin as she squealed with joy then set her down again.

Zane thought Evan's mom and dad were friendly. Both

welcomed him into their home, which he found fascinating. The inventions continued as much inside the home as he had seen outside on the streets.

Walls were lined with odd contraptions, some working as wheels spun as they immitted squeaks, while others stood still. Some had parts missing, in a current disarray of disuse and others were only skeletons of their previous forms.

Evan explained about the Z-rider and both his parents wanted to see the rider and its diagram Zane had drawn. They bent over the drawing and then asked several questions about the functionality of the rider.

"It's just used as a single person cart." Evan explained and turned to Zane as if waiting for him to confirm this.

"Er, yes. I use it to travel around my hub." Zane didn't mention how the rider had actually been invented to zip illegally around the undergrown rails in the Pipes.

"The council will want to keep a copy of the plans; did you make your own copy just in case they keep this one?" Evan's mother asked.

With a fresh copy of the Z-rider's plans and Evan's dad along for the ride, they used the school's cart to drive down to the offices of the council. Zane had brought his Z-rider to show the council a finished product and found he was suddenly nervous.

The building the council's offices were in was a vast white building which sat in the hub's center. The tallest building by far, that had its entryway littered with working and broken inventions. Zane saw a moving sidewalk and steps that fascinated him. He wanted a closer look, but Evan waved his hand and tugged on Zane's arm to get him moving in the right direction.

"We can play later." Evan hissed.

They had to wait twenty minutes before they were allowed in to see the council which was made of six men and six women. Each councilmember had grey hair and smile on their faces. A young clerk sat before them typing on an electric machine with each word spoken.

Zane tried to explain his Z-rider and after giving Evan a painful look, was glad when his friend took over with the rider's details while Zane demonstrated the rider by zipping all over the room.

When they returned to the Academy that night, Zane had a freshly stamped seal of authenticity and permit to sell his Z-riders. He quickly made a copy of both and sent it to Mia, along with half of the credits he had earned so far. He had given the other half to Rafe and Miles for supplies.

When both boys finally returned two hours after Evan and he had, they were dirty but smiling. Soot covered Rafe and Miles had a big rip on the knee of his pants.

"We found the wheels easy enough, but the circuits were hard to locate." Rafe explained with a sigh.

"Had to climb all over the pile of electrical boards before we found some." Miles said and swiped his forehead, successfully smearing more soot on his face.

"So, you found three?" Zane asked.

"Actually, we found twenty." Rafe replied and lifted the sack and dumped its contents on the desk.

"Twenty?" Zane asked as some of the circuit boards spilled onto the floor.

"We didn't use all the credits either." Miles informed them. "And we got that many wheels too, they're out in the cart still."

FUN

Zane and his four friends spent their free time bent over the large table set in the center of their dorm room while they built Z-riders. When they weren't working on schoolwork, eating or sleeping, they were building.

Beside the three riders they were building for Delany's aunt and friends, they had eight more orders from classmates. Word traveled fast after the first few orders and before the third quarter was over, they had several more orders, some from students and three from staff members including the Dean's assistant, Sarah.

Zane still had his tutor meetings with Mitch which he appreciated as his coding lessons were getting harder. They were now learning about circuits which ran the air vents in each hub. Zane knew about the leading boards that ran the pipes, but air vents were a different matter as they included filters and holding tanks. It wasn't the usually easy open/close function and once again, Zane found himself struggling to comprehend these lessons.

Government class was another struggle of his too. The professor kept talking about sub-committees and loved to drone on about small details that were always found in the section's tests at the end of each week.

Environmentalist class and Architect class were two of the easiest, at least for him. Rafe struggled in Architect class and feared he wouldn't receive a passing grade.

"Mom's not going to be pleased." Rafe said one evening as he bent over his e-tablet.

"What are you struggling with?" Zane asked as he stood from his own tablet to stretch his legs.

"Everything!" Rafe said in a quick explosion. "I don't understand why I need to know what's holding up a building as long as it's still standing!"

The frustration in Rafe's voice made Zane smile as he neared his friend. If Rafe was struggling, then it made him feel better about his own troubles with schoolwork.

"Oh, this one." Zane said with a smile as he looked at the detailed drawing of the underbelly of a building. "I might be able to help. See, here, this beam runs along the pipes. Well, down in the pipes you just can't bend them around the structure, the structure must move around the pipes. That way you don't interrupt the flow the pipes provide."

"You've been down in the pipes?" Rafe's question had Zane subconsciously nodding before he stopped and turned his eyes towards his friend. "No." He hissed and shook his head, but he knew it was already too late, his secret was out.

"You have!" Rafe's excited voice caused the other two to come over.

"What's going on?" Evan asked.

"Z's been down in the pipes!" Rafe blurted out to Zane's horror.

"No!" Zane urged.

"You have." Rafe demanded and pointed at him. "I can see it in your eyes."

Feeling frustrated and knowing he couldn't lie anymore, Zane quickly dashed up to shut the door to their dorm. "No, I haven't. Shh. Someone will hear."

"So? What's the big deal?" Miles questioned as Zane rushed over and turned on his music pod. He then motioned his friends over near the machine as it emitted pops and zaps in mid song from the approved school station.

"The big deal is I'm not supposed to go down there." Zane explained as he sat on his bed in defeat.

"So, you have been down there." Rafe confirmed with a smile.

"Yes, loads." Zane replied with a shake of his head. He felt all his fear of being discovered melt away as he faced his friends. He trusted these three boys, he knew if he explained his hidden past, they would understand and keep his secrets.

"Why the secrets?" Evan asked with a shrug of his shoulders.

"The problem is, seeing as I don't have a father, I'm not allowed down there. It's illegal." Zane said with frustration, he knew he would share his explorations of the pipes but knew he must still hold back the horrors of that last night in the pipes. His witnessing the death of the unknown man was a secret he must keep, always. "But I used to sneak down there and explore."

"What are they like? You told us they're dangerous,

weren't you scared exploring them?" Evan asked as he leaned forward with excitement all over his dark face.

Quietly and quickly Zane explained about the pipes. He told them how his Z-rider had originally been a rail-rider and how he would zip along the rails for hours. He told of the vastness of the pipes down under their feet. How a whole world was located there, miles and miles of vastness that was only seen by a few of the inhabitance of ECHO.

"It sounds unbelievable." Rafe uttered with a shake of his head.

"It sounds amazing!" Evan corrected. "We should go there!"

"What?" Miles said with a shake of his head. "Why?"

"Don't you see, it's part of our world, we have to go!" Evan urged with conviction. "Z, you could take us!"

"No, he can't. We are two hubs away from the pipes." Miles quickly said.

"No, they're underneath us." Evan argued.

"You can't get to the pipes from here." Miles stated trying to sound bored, but Zane heard fear in his voice.

"Actually, there are hatches everywhere." Zane's words had all three boys looking at him again.

"You know where a hatch is?" Rafe asked with excitement.

"Of course. I explored all the pipes." Zane explained with another shake of his head.

"You, I mean could you take us down there?" Evan asked as excitement covered his face.

"Why, why do you want to go down there?" Zane asked, all of a sudden confused by his friend's interest. He could understand if they wanted to go to the main hub, maybe see the wonders there, but the pipes, they were just dirty and dangerous.

"Why did you explore them?" Rafe's question brought Zane's mind back to his friend. "How long did you explore the pipes, why did you keep going back?"

Shrugging his shoulders, Zane thought for a moment. "Because they were there, and they were forbidden to me."

A slow smile spread on Rafe and Evan's face as they nodded their head in agreement. Only Miles looked doubtful as he stood there with his arms crossed over his chest, but after a moment he too smiled.

"Well, why not." Miles finally said with a laugh. "It will be a kick."

THEY PLANNED for their forbidding trip down into the pipes the rest of that night. Zane called the shots as to when they would sneak down. It had to be at night, and it would have to be in total secret.

"No one must know." Zane urged his friends. "Ever!"

"We understand." Rafe confirmed.

"Not tonight or tomorrow." Zane explained, we have too much schoolwork, and we are set to deliver three Z-riders tomorrow night." He explained as Evan nodded quickly and nodded his own head.

"When?" Evan demanded, and frustration and impatience filled his friend's voice.

"Three nights time." Zane said and leaned closer to his friends. "We have some prep. Did you bring your chest plates?"

Two of his friends shook their head to Zane's frustration, only Evan had nodded.

"No, we really don't use them much." Rafe said with a shake of his head. "Mostly we use them for parades."

"Fixers use them when they're on a job." Evan said and moved over to his closet to pull out his chest plate.

"I don't have one." Miles said with a shake of his head.

"What?" Zane asked shocked as he turned to study his friend.

"Never needed one." Miles replied making Zane think of the vast differences of the hubs once again.

"We have head lamps." Rafe said and after walking over to his closet, returned with two odd straps held together with a square light. "Mostly I use it to read after you guys go to bed."

"I have one of those too." Evan provided and moved to collect his.

"Good, you and Miles can wear those. Evan and I will wear our Chest plates for light." Zane explained. "We have to limit our time down in the pipes, I know this hub's pipes well, there is a Pod stored nearby so I can show you that, also there's a control panel room, I think you'll want to see that. That should take about an hour to get to if we bring the Z-riders."

After the plan was set, they kept quiet about their intentions. Zane could tell that Evan was impatient for the three days to pass. He kept tapping his foot during quiet times, as if he was trying to urge time to pass faster.

Zane understood his friend's impatience, he too was excited to return to the pipes. His times exploring by himself seemed years ago, and part of him yearned to share the underworld with his new friends.

Zane didn't dare tell Mitch about his plans to return to the pipes. He knew Mitch wouldn't understand the need to return down into the pipes, that and Mitch wouldn't trust Zane's bunk friends. Mitch, these days, didn't appear to trust anyone. Zane knew his friend had a reason, after all it was Mitch's own mother who had tried to turn Zane into the Primary.

The three days passed and with it came Terraform day. Zane had scheduled their secret adventure for the same night that all hubs celebrated the day that ECHO had landed on the planet Amara and the vast machines had started the long and vast transformation to the world outside.

Each hub celebrated differently, but they all did celebrate. Celebrations for this holiday usually included a mid-day party in the streets.

Zane wanted to use the day's events to prepare for their nightly excursion. He knew lessons were halted the next day, much like New Year's Day, and hoped they could enter the pipes and travel to and from the hatch without discovery.

For the Academy, the main celebration took place in the Kitchen hall. Food and sweets were plentiful. Zane and his friends spent time with Breanna and Ash along with several others. Zane had fun talking and laughing with his friends and actually found himself relaxing when his mind was distracted from the expectations of the coming night's adventures.

After the party, which lasted well past the evening mealtime, the four walked back to their dorm. They hadn't used their Z-riders that day, having kept them on their charging stations to ensure they had plenty of battery power for their evening's adventures.

"When?" Evan whined as soon as their dorm room door was closed.

"Twenty-three hundred." Zane replied and felt the same frustration that Evan displayed. Such a long wait seemed to last. The boys played games, read and even tried throwing a disc around the room at each other while trying to make the time pass more quickly.

When the hour drew closer, Zane had them change into dark clothing and he and Evan slipped into their chest plates.

"When we leave the room, no one talks. No matter what. If you need to communicate, use hand signals." He warned. "Stay close. And remember, when we're down in the pipes, touch nothing! Nothing. Ask me if you have questions, but only do as I tell you."

Each of his friends nodded and they all quietly slipped out of the room, each carrying their Z-riders. Since Zane's still fit on the back of his chest plate, this left his hands free, so he was the one who closed and opened the doors.

They moved past their building and down the block to where Zane had spotted the hatch the first day he had arrived. Upon seeing the hatch, he had known its subterranean location immediately.

The Academy hub had been one of his favorite hubs to explore and also one of the simplest. Its pipes and tunnels were in vast squares, each lined with the prior square, unlike the Fixer hub which held more turns and twists than even the main hub had.

Now, after using his hand tool to loosen the hatch, he motioned his friends to slip quickly down the ladder.

After Miles had vanished down, he followed and

closed the hatch behind, making sure to keep the handle opened. After the latch had closed, he clicked on his chest plate. His blue piper light mixed with Evan's orange after his friend had turned his on, then it combined with the pale white of the headlamps.

He reached the bottom of the ladder and found his three friends waiting for him. Excitement of the unknown all over their faces.

"Ok, we have three tunnels to travers before we see the rails. Once we get there, remember, don't touch the rails. Even though its night, there may still be power left running along them." Zane explained. "Stay to the side, if you fall behind, give a shout. Sound carries down here, but no one should be inside the tunnels this late. So only shout if you need help."

Zane unlatched his Z-rider and turned it on. He saw his friends copy his movements and after nodding, took off riding his machine down the darkened tunnels.

At each junction Zane stopped and checked on his friends. Rafe had a grin on his face and Evan's eyes seemed to bounce around in his head as he tried to look at everything.

On the third stop, Zane guided them over to a pipe junction and spent a few minutes explaining the functionality of the tubes. Miles had several questions about the circuit boards that ran the controls and when Zane looked at the time on his chest plate, he was shocked to see fifteen minutes had passed.

"The next tunnel will house the Pod and the rails. Remember, don't touch anything without asking first." Zane urged and then headed down the tunnel on the right.

His friends found the rail pod interesting. Rafe studied it and mentioned that it was similar to the carts used in the main hub.

"They run along the high rail which runs across the hub." Rafe informed them. "You can see it each time you enter the hub."

"My dad used to work on that, it's how he got the idea for his Leviathan."

Zane spent ten minutes showing them the pod, then he had them speeding along another tunnel aiming for the control panel room. It took them eight minutes to reach the room. When they arrived, Zane was confused to see a lock blocked their entrance to the room.

"This is new." He said as he picked up the lock and studied it. "Wasn't here before."

"Why would it be locked?" Miles asked.

Shaking his head, Zane turned to look at his friends. "No clue." He replied and scratched his head.

"What else could we see?" Evan asked.

"I think that should be it. We have to get back." He saw disappointment in his friends faces, but something about the new lock had worry growing in him.

What if the lock was there because of what had happened down in the pipes several months ago? All of a sudden Mia's warnings came back to him. Her insistence about him not returning to the pipes echoed in his mind as he looked at his friends.

"Stay close, remember, two lefts and four rights to get back to the hatch."

His uneasy feeling increased when they drew near to the rail pod. When he saw a flash down one of the side tunnels he quickly turned his chest plate off, his friends quickly followed his lead and soon they all were stopped on their Z-riders in the blackness of the tunnels.

He felt Rafe bump into the back of him and he gave his friend's hand a squeeze which signaled him to grab Evan's hand, who then would grab Miles. After their odd chain was formed, Zane moved forward a little until he could make out a form down the side tunnel.

It was the light he saw first, but then the sound of footsteps could be heard, they were drawing near. Tugging Rafe's arm, he had his friends all reach down and grab their Z-riders, after he slipped his on his pack, he felt Rafe's hand slap down on his left shoulder and knew the others were now linked by one hand on the other's shoulders while their free hand carried their riders.

Zane knew a hidden panel was near, but he feared that all four boys wouldn't fit inside the small cube. The only other option would be to try and reach the far tunnel leading out of the pipes before the person could find them. He knew there was a different hatch than the one they had used before, it was one tunnel over, but it would grant them access out of the pipes.

Making up his mind, he turned quickly around and had them heading towards the new hatch at a quick pace. To his horror, he saw that the light was gaining on them and quickened his pace.

Who was down here? Were there patrols now down in the pipes during the night hours?

Fear had sweat trickling down his back as he felt Rafe's strong grip on his shoulder. This reminded him he wasn't the only person in danger of being caught, what would happen to his friends if they were caught down here?

He didn't fear being kicked out of the Academy, but his friends didn't' have an unknown donor protecting them from this fate.

When he saw the outline of the hatch ladder, he urged Rafe up quickly and then Evan and last Miles.

Without a light, Miles fought to gain the first rung and Zane heard his friend grunt loudly. The sound seemed to reverberate in the vast darkness and the unknown footsteps seemed to quicken.

Before the light could penetrate the tunnel he and his friends were trying to escape from, Zane had a quick glance of blood oozing out of Mile's forehead before he shoved his friend upwards.

As they reached the open hatch, he shoved Mile's legs out and then followed him and quickly closed the hatch behind.

"Quickly!" Zane said as he stood and reached for his Z-rider. "Back to the dorm."

"Miles is hurt." Evan exclaimed; his voice no longer sounded excited but scared.

"Quickly, can he ride?" Zane asked and saw through the dim light that blood now trailed down his friend's face. He breathed a breath of relief when he saw Mile's eyes opened and he nodded once.

"Back to the dorm, we'll clean you up there." Zane urged and they once again hoped on their Z-riders.

Two blocks from their building Mile's fell off his rider. Thankfully, he landed in a bush, but the blood running down his head left a smear along the stones as his friends' half dragged, half carried him along the pathways towards safety.

When they reached their dorm, Zane saw that the gash

along Mile's head was deep and his friend was very pale and when he closed his eyes, he was unresponsive. Zane quickly ran to Tyler and after waking their dorm advisor, told him Mile's had fallen off his Z-rider and hit his head.

The nurse was one again called and before she had arrived, all the lights and chest plates had been quickly stashed and their story was set.

"We went on a night ride and Miles crashed his rider a block over." Rafe informed her when she asked how the accident had happened when they were supposed to be in their beds.

"There was too much blood." Evan replied, his own face pale as he looked down at their unconscious friend.

"A doctor will have to be called; this boy needs stitches." She informed them and studied their dark clothing. "Where did this happen?"

"I can show you." Zane said, and was thankful the scene where Miles had crashed a block away would provide proof of their above ground accident.

"That will not be necessary, but why were you boys out of bed?" She asked, a frown on her plump face.

"That's my fault." Tyler said quickly as all eyes turned to him. "I wanted to see how the Z-riders would work in the dark. I thought it would be fun." The lie from the dorm advisor had earned another frown from the nurse, but she voiced no more questions.

WORK

*M*iles ended up with ten stitches running along his broad forehead. His mother had been the doctor who had sewn him up. She had then proceeded to scold him and his friends extensively for being out of bed and for riding a dangerous machine in the dark. Evan appeased her by telling her he was currently inventing a protection cap that would be worn when riding the Z-rider.

"It will save his brain from injury." He urged then showed her his quickly drawn sketch of the cap he had been working on since they returned to the dorm that night.

"Be that as it may, I don't want him riding that thing until after your invention is finished and I personally inspect it." She frowned down at the drawing and turned to study Evan. "It will need a strap, so it stays on the head." She advised and then quickly turned to study her son. "No school until after you are cleared. That means screen time too. Your head and brain need to heal."

It took four days before Miles was allowed back to classes, by then his nightly adventure was the talk of the school.

"I heard his brains leaked out all over the walkway." Manny said with an exaggerated laugh during Base class the day after Miles had returned. "Nothing left inside from what I heard." This statement was followed by many laughs.

"He still has more than you, then." Zane said confidently as he followed Miles to their seat. This statement had scowls and leers aimed his way, but Zane was rewarded when Miles gave a chuckle.

True to their word, none of the boys rode their Z-rider until Evan's safety cap had been completed. The fixer made a quick run home on the next free day and filed his own stamped seal of authenticity and then received a permit to sell his Safe caps as he called them. Each boy had built their own cap using Evan's specifications.

Rafe covered his with stickers he had found in a store from the main hub. Zane painted his cap a bright green and blue which reminded him of the paintings he had marveled at. Evan had mounted his light on his and Miles kept his cap a plan black.

Soon, students could be seen zipping around the courtyards and pathways, each on a Z-rider and each wearing brightly decorated caps. Even Breanna had joined in the fun, after buying her own Z-rider and receiving a private lesson from Zane.

He had taken pleasure and embarrassment in showing her how to stand on the board. His face had turned a bright red when he had helped her keep a steady stance by placing his hands on her elbows and one time, on her waist, which had earned him a big smile from her.

The fourth quarter was quickly approaching, and students found the times for fun soon diminished as warnings of test finals sounded around the halls and classrooms. Usually the evenings were spent on personal matters, but most students now found themselves staying up past their normal bedtimes to get in a few more studying hours.

Homework littered their lives and made several students cracked under the emotional stress. For the 'level one' students the pressure was hardest. Never had they been put through the paces of finals and only the warnings from parents and professors kept them from slacking in their studies.

For Zane, there was no exception. Despite his knowledge that he was assured a return for Level two training, he focused and worked hard for each class. His grades had dipped and swayed confirming the Dean wasn't allowing the professors to override his true grades per their agreement.

After his grades dipped low, he would then quickly go to the professor of that class and asked for extra credit assignments. He knew all the professors allowed this for other students too, so he didn't feel this practice was excluded to others.

The week of Zane's birthday was a particularly rough one. Third quarter grades had been sent out and parents were scheduled to hold meetings with the professors the entire week. These meetings were set to discuss the student's goals regarding either their next level year or in the case of higher leveled students, jobs.

Zane was excited that Mia would travel over to the hub for these meetings, and also join him for a quick birthday celebration. They had planned the meetings so she would have her afternoon free and they could take a cart over to the main hub for some much-deserved shopping.

Zane had been looking online at a new sewing machine for Mia and hoped to use the credits he had earned by selling Z-riders. Credits from the sale of the riders had been constantly pouring in. The production of the riders still kept all four boys busy on their free days. Zane, with the help of Evan, had created a working contract with his friends, this also meant they all shared in the profits of the business.

Mia arrival was two days before Zane's birthday but that didn't dampen his spirits. The first meeting she had was with the Dean himself. Zane knew the other parents didn't have a private meeting with Head Dean Dickson and assumed this meeting was due to his special circumstances. He wasn't disappointed when the Dean poured praises on Zane about his dedication to his schoolwork.

Next, they met with his professors in order of his classes. At one point he saw Mitch and his mom walking along the corridors, but quickly grabbed Mia's hand to prevent her from calling out to Melony. He still hadn't forgiven her for giving the Primary his name in connection to the witness of the murder.

After their last meeting, Zane grabbed a cart and drove them out of the Academy hub and into the Prime hub for a special treat. Rafe had drawn directions for Zane and he quickly found the little café his friend had been told about.

"Rafe says they have excellent coffee and biscuits here." Zane explained as he helped Mia out of the school's cart.

"Zane, this is nice, but I don't need to be treated, it's your birthday not mine." Mia replied as she tried to straighten the home sewn orange skirt she wore. She had a buttoned cream-colored top and wore her prettiest shawl over her shoulders. To Zane, she reminded him of home and thought she looked great.

He saw her fluff up her hair once before they entered the Café and smiled as her eyes opened wide as she scanned all the selections behind the counters.

They drank imitation creamed coffee and had little finger sandwiches in the pretty stripped chairs which were set about the store. Mia laughed at Zane's jokes and told him all about the news from home.

They then walked two store fronts down and watched as once again Mia's eyes grew large when she saw the sewing machine, he had already purchased online for her.

"Mr. Donson here is going to give you a lesson on this machine." Zane explained as Mia stroked the shiny device with her hands.

"Oh, I don't want to be a bother." Mia said with a wave of her hand.

"Nonsense, it's all part of the service." Mr. Donson, a rather small but friendly man explained as he pulled out a chair for Mia to sit in. "I must say, that is an extraordinary pretty shawl, where did you buy it?"

"This thing?" Mia said with a smile and Zane saw his grandmother blush for the first time in a long time. "I made it."

The sewing machine tutorial went on for an hour. At the end Mia knew how to run her new machine, and also had twenty orders for shawls that Mr. Donson seemed rather pleased about.

"Mia, you know you could have charged him twice that much and he would have paid it." Zane said with a shake of his head as they walked back to the cart.

"Nonsense, why would I charge that much, it only costs me a fraction of what he is paying to make them." Mia's words were interrupted when three tall figures blocked their path to the cart.

"Well, well, boys, looks who's trying to move up in the world?" The sound of Weston's voice had Zane's eyes narrowing as he studied the three.

Zane was currently carrying Mia's new machine, which weighted about twenty pounds. He knew he couldn't drop it to defend himself, so he slowly handed it to Mia. When she took the device without question, he knew she understood the danger they currently were in.

As he glanced at all three boys who stood blocking their way forward, he saw other people walking past. This was a crowded street; surly Weston and his goons wouldn't attack him and his grandmother on a crowded street.

"What do you want?" Zane demanded as he tried to push Mia behind him. He met with some resistance as his grandmother stood her ground.

"If you boys will excuse me and my grandson, we have some more shopping to do." Mia stated in a ton Zane knew usually was reserved for rather stupid people.

"Trying to buy your way up in the world, are you?" Omar sneered, his dark face menacing as he took another step forward.

"How dare you," Mia started but stopped when Zane stepped in front of her.

"I suggest you three head back to school before the Dean hears about this." Zane said, already poised on the balls of his feet ready for any trouble the three might cause.

"My dad already talked to the Dean, turns out dad wasn't pleased with the special treatment some low lifers are getting. It appears things will change after today." Weston sneered and bumped his finger against Zane's chest. "You may need to watch your step from now on."

"I always have to around you three; I don't want any of your foul stench to stick to me." Zane mocked with a smile. He then quickly used one hand to push Mia backwards as Omar's fist swung out at him from the side and Weston raised his own fists to join the fight.

He heard Mia scream and felt Weston's fist connect with his midriff. Omar's punch had gone wide, but his next swing hit Zane directly above his left ear. Using his own fist, Zane felt satisfaction when he heard a crunch from Weston's nose and saw blood pour from it.

'Probably broken again.' Zane thought before he saw another fist coming right at him. Ducking, he felt the blow miss his face and glance off his right temple before he raised his arms and landed two blows directly into Manny's face. The tall boy fell backwards clutching his battered face as Omar bent his head and charged at Zane.

Knowing if he dodged Omar, the kid might go barreling into Mia, who still stood behind him, Zane used his arms to grab him around his shoulders after he had already slammed into Zane's stomach. Giving a quick pivot he had Omar thrown to the ground and his arms up for Weston's next assault.

"Stop it this instant!" Came a deep voice which all four boys successfully ignored.

Zane had his hands up and was blocking Weston's next hit before it registered that the kid was no longer attacking him. Peeking between his raised hands he saw Weston was currently being held two feet off the ground by a very large man.

"That is enough!" Came the deep voice again. Zane felt Mia's arms wrapped around him and watched as Weston's feet started to kick out in the struggle against the giant man.

"You three are detained." Said the man as he continued to hold Weston feet above the ground. "I have already called the nearest Forcer on duty. You there, you better stay on the ground if you know what's good for you." The man growled and pointed at Manny who still sat upon the ground holding his face. "Are you two alright?"

The question was thrown at Zane and Mia so quickly that neither responded until the large man asked a second time.

"Yes, I think so." Zane finally replied and turned to study Mia. "They didn't hurt you, did they?"

"No, but I dropped my new machine." She said with a shudder and turned back to their rescuer. "Thank you…"

"Forcer Carrington." The man supplied as he continued to hold Weston tightly by the arm.

He set the boy down but the look on his face indicated he wanted to pick him up again and shake him a few more times. Forcer Carrington was a large man about six five.

His short, buzzed dark hair had hints of grey about the temples. Sharp blue eyes studied Mia and Zane from below straight eyebrows. When the left brow raised a bit, Zane saw the man smile and he appeared less threatening to him because of it.

"Thank you, Forcer Carrington." Mia said again as she bent to retrieve her new Sewing machine.

"Here Mia, let me get that." Zane said quickly and picked up the device. "I don't think it broke."

"If it is, these three will pay for any damages." Forcer Carrington stated as sounds of many feet could be heard running down the pathway. "Over here Grantson, I have the three who caused this scuffle."

Forcer Carrington turned out to be off duty at the moment and had witnessed Weston and Omar launch their attack. He had quickly called for his team's aid and then arrived in time to save Zane from any further punches.

"Not that you couldn't handle yourself." Forcer Carrington said with a smile aimed at Zane.

"Thank you again Forcer…"

"Please, call me Brad." He interjected and smiled down at Mia. For the second time that day Zane saw his grandmother blush.

"Thank you Brad." Mia said. "I am so glad you were here to help."

"Any time. Please let me help you to your cart." After Brad helped Mia settle her new machine into the school's cart, he gave her his private card in case there was any damage. He and his men had taken Mia and Zane's contact information and said the report would be sent to them within a day.

After their adventure, Zane took Mia straight home. He had hoped to take her shopping to the fabric store, one Rafe had given him directions to, but felt they had had enough adventure for one day.

"You make sure and message me as soon as you get back to your dorm. I worry about those three boys trying to attack you again." Mia said.

"Mia, I don't think Forcer Carrington will let them out of his sight for a several hours." Zane said and tilted his head in confusion when he saw Mia blush again.

The ride back to school was a quick one. Zane left the e-cart near his dorm and found all three of his bunk mates back in their room.

"Z, Dean Dickson was looking for you." Evan stated when he walked in the room. "His assistant asked if you could return to his office."

"What did you do now?" Rafe asked as he studied Zane's scraped knuckles.

"Met with our friends in the main hub." Zane explained as he quickly switched back to his school uniform. "But they met with a large Forcer after tasting my fists."

He had only a minute to explain the adventure he and Mia had in the main hub before he raced back out of the room and headed to the Dean's office. He used the same e-cart he had used the entire day and Sarah waved him right in when he arrived.

"Zane!" Dean Dickson said with a large wave of his beefy hand. "Please, come on in."

Zane was halfway in the room before he saw the slender figure woman sitting in one of the Dean's chairs.

When Primary Kasher stood, Zane's heart froze in his chest and his mouth grew dry.

She was taller than she looked on the screens. Her blond hair reminded him of Breanna's but the cool eyes that studied him did not. Breanna had her mother's nose and coloring, but there was no warmth or welcome in this woman's face.

"Hello Mr. Noman. You are a hard boy to lock down for a meeting." Primary Kasher said and he saw that the smile she gave him only touched her lips.

"Please, come sit down." Dean Dickson said as he waved one of his beefy hands at an empty chair.

The legs Zane walked on wanted to shake, but he was grateful he made it to the chair without falling. His eyes remained on the Primary just like hers remained on him.

"I was concerned when I heard that one of your dorm mates was injured a while ago." Primary Kasher started as she tilted her head slightly. "I heard he was injured during night games."

Giving no response, Zane continued to sit still. His mind flashed to that night and now understood that someone had been patrolling the Pipes. He should have listened to Mia and stayed away, but the hint of adventure had been too much for him and his friends.

"Tell me," Primary Kasher leaned forward and placed her slender hands on the knees of her pants as she continued to study him. "How did you find the pipes that night."

"I'm not allowed in the pipes." Zane stated and hoped he sounded convincing. The new smile on Kasher's face told him she didn't believe him.

"Are you telling me it's a coincidence that the same

night my guards chased an intruder out of the pipes you and your friends had an accident? There was blood on the stairs leading up to this hub." Kasher exclaimed and her eyes narrowed a fraction.

Not knowing how to answer Zane used his own curiosity as a shield.

"I don't know anything about an intruder. Maybe you should ask Waltson." Zane was pleased to see fear bloomed in the woman's eyes.

When she leaned back, Zane saw her hands tighten on her knees before she nodded and smiled once more.

"No longer mild." She whispered so faintly that Zane wasn't sure he had heard her correctly. "Know this." She said as she stood and looked down at him. "The Pipes are off limits to everyone not authorized. If you, or anyone you know, trespasses again, they will be caught and prosecuted."

Zane found it hard to swallow as he sat there looking up at Breanna's mother. Did she know, did she understand he and her daughter were friends? Did she know Mitch and he were friends? That it was he who had witnessed the death of the mysterious man many months ago?

Zane worried that the answer was yes as she continued to study him.

"Despite my advice you have been brought here." She said and leaned forward over Zane. Her nose inches from his as she glanced at him with cruel eyes. "For now."

DISCOVERIES

Zane didn't sleep that night. Nor the next.

His dorm mates wanted to hear details of his adventures in the main hub and Evan marveled each time Zane told of Weston being held aloft by the tall Forcer Carrington.

"I've heard of him." Rafe supplied after the first telling. "He's like you Zane." Confused by his friend's words Zane quickly was told that Brad had no father. "His mother's father was pretty high in the government, so he had Brad's name changed to his mother's. That's why he's not a Carringson." Rafe supplied.

"You can do that? You can change your name?" Zane asked, amazed at this information.

"Well, it's not common, but yeah." Rafe said with a smile.

Zane messaged Mia the next day and told her about his meeting with Primary Kasher. He wasn't shocked that after his classes, he found a message pod waiting in his dorm from her.

As Mia's worried voice sounded out of the pod urging him to refrain from going down into the Pipes again, his guilt at disobeying her increased. She told him it had been smart using Waltson's name and asked if he had discovered anything more on his unknown donor.

He returned the pod with a definite No and a solum promise to not set a foot down in the pipes again.

His birthday was spent in classes and that night he and his friends celebrated in the kitchen hall. Breanna gave him a small gift of a cool drawing she had done. Since it reminded him of the landscape paintings, he hung it on his pod's wall above his bed.

Evan gave him a cool sticker that he immediately placed on his safety cap and he got a replacement chin strap from Miles. He was excited about the gift Rafe gave him. The new jacket wasn't black like the one he had, but a thin brown jacket that had a big orange Z on the back.

"I figure you could wear it when you're riding." Rafe said with a shrug of his broad shoulders.

Zane's birthday was made even better when he heard over dinner what had happened to Weston and his cronies.

"They aren't expelled, but I heard their parents had to attend a hearing." Evan explained as he munched on his slice of protein cake.

"Hearing?" Zane asked as a quick feeling of joy filled him.

"Yeah, remember we learned about it in the first quarter of government class." Breanna said with a smile. "Their parents had to represent their child and the arresting Forcer and victim had to be present."

Zane thought of Mia and frowned. "I wasn't there." He murmured.

"Well, no. I guess your grandmother went instead. We had class, which is why all three boys missed lessons. I suspect they will be back tomorrow." Breanna said with a nod of her head.

Weston and his friends appeared back at school two days after Zane's birthday. Each gave him a sour look but avoided being close to him, which gave him hope that their attempts to ambush him would finally end.

Each night of the final quarter of school Zane would study and each morning the professors would find a new assignment to thrust upon him. About the time Zane felt his brains might leak out of his head the finals arrived.

Sleepless nights were met with long days. Tests and the essay questions filled his mind long after he was finished. He worried about his answers and his future. He had nightmares about coding and fretted that even with all his extra credit, he would still fail his courses.

What could a fatherless boy of fifteen do for a job with only a level one education? He knew he would always have a home with Mia but being an errand boy for the rest of his life was no way to make a living.

With all the studying, Zane thought the end of school zipped by way too quickly. The day of his final test came and went. After his last class, Zane sat down on the steps of the environmentalist building and put his head in his hands.

"Feels good to get them all done." Evan stated with a large sigh as he plopped down next to Zane.

"What?" Zane asked, looking up at his friend.

"Dad tells me even if I fail, they are going to pay for me

to redo level one." Evan explained with a smile and a wink. "Of course, I know for sure I passed four of my classes. It was Government class that I struggled with."

"You don't have to worry about that." Breanna said as she sat on the other side of Zane. "Level twos don't need to take that if they don't want to."

"Really?" Evan asked with hope on his face.

"Of course, I have to take it for five more years." She said with a frown. "What with my mom and all."

"Are we having a party here?" Rafe asked as he and Miles walked up and joined them on the steps.

"Just trying to cheer up the kid." Evan explained as he slapped Zane on his back.

"Don't worry, I'm sure you did great." Rafe said and then shook his head. "Of course, I might have failed Architect class."

"No way, did you see the questions on the foundations? After our little night trip, I think all of us got that right." Miles said as Zane and Rafe quickly tried to quiet their friend.

"Night trip?" Breanna asked as she squinted her eyes at the boys.

"Nothing." Miles said and tried to wave off her questions.

"I knew it was more than just a Z-rider accident." Breanna hissed.

"It was nothing." Rafe said and quickly looked at her. "Zane just took us around to show us some foundations. That's all."

Zane wasn't sure if Breanna believed him or not. But since her mother already suspected him and his friends of going down into the Pipes, he didn't worry much if Breanna guessed what had really happened.

"Come one, I'm starving." Zane urged and tugged on Breanna's hand to pull her up off the stairs.

"Zane, what will you do on break?" Breanna asked him.

"I guess I'll head home and help Mia with her deliveries again." He replied with a shrug of his shoulders and tried to fight the depression that wanted to settle in his chest. "You?"

After a large sigh, Breanna spoke of shadowing her mother at her job for the two months they would be away from school.

"How about you, Rafe?" Zane asked his friend.

"Well, since my dad died, I will have to shadow my grandfather, but I can't do that this year, so I'll have the two months free." Rafe said and mirrored Zane's shrug.

"When did your father die?" Breanna asked.

"Just before school. That's why I started at the Academy. My mom and her new husband wanted to send me for formal education." Rafe supplied. "Of course, I was already signed up when they found dad. But I was a day late because of the funeral."

Something in Zane's mind buzzed as he walked alongside his friend. The more Rafe talked about his father, the louder the noise became.

"Found him?" Zane heard his weak voice ask as he stopped along the pathway.

"Yeah, they found him in a sublevel of the main hub. That's one of the reasons why I wanted to, well you know..." Rafe said with another shrug of his shoulders.

Turning, Zane studied his friend as if seeing him for

the first time. He saw Rafe's strong chin, his straight nose and thick eyebrows and an image flashed across his eyes of the dying man. Yes, there were similarities between the two. Rafe wasn't as old as the dying man, of course, but there were definite resemblances.

Was Rafe's father the man he had seen die all those months ago? Had he been living with the man's son the whole time? How had he not known he had been so close to the answer the whole time?

Tugging on Rafe's arm, he stopped as the others continued towards the kitchen hall.

"Rafe, your father, who was he?" Zane whispered his question as Rafe stopped next to him and turned to study him.

"I'm Rafe Hudson." Rafe explained and tried to smile at Zane. "I live with my mother and step-dad, but Hudson Adamson was my dad."

A buzzing in Zane's ears grew loud as the image of the old man standing in the doorway of his hospital room swam before his eyes. Adam, the man he had met in the Piper hub before school had started said he was a friend of Mia's, but was he Rafe's grandfather?"

Clearing his throat, Zane asked the question that was burning in his mind. "Who is Waltson?"

"Adam Waltson?" Rafe looked confused at first, then smiled. "He's my grandpa."

ZANE'S DISCOVERIES of the dead man's name, Hudson, along with who Adam Waltson was, was mind boggling. He stood there in the middle of the pathway as his world tilted around him. New questions sprung to his mind giving him an instant headache.

"Why are you asking about grandpa?" Rafe wanted to know.

Shaking his pounding head, Zane's mind was too full of questions to provide an answer at this time. After shrugging his shoulders, he mumbled something about Mia knowing him.

Rafe shrugged his shoulders again and turned to follow the others to the Kitchen hall. Zane wasn't shocked to discover his previous appetite gone.

His headache was soon accompanied by a sour feeling in the pit of his stomach. He couldn't tell Rafe that he had been present the night his father had died. That the man had actually died in his arms was something only he, Mia and Mitch knew.

If anyone else found out his secret, Zane worried their freedom would been gone. The prisons loomed over him as he thought of Forcers coming to claim him, Mia and poor little Mitch.

The smug face of Primary Kasher filled his face as he sat there at the table with his friends. Only Breanna noticed he was quiet, he hoped she thought he was worried about his grades. There was no way she could guess the horrific truth.

How had he lived so long with Rafe and not know it was his friend's father that had died down in the pipes? As he sat there quietly, he remembered his prior resolution to find out about his friend's lives. He had foolishly started with Evan which had resulted in discovery that had side-tracked him regarding the differences between the hubs.

A difference and discovery that had resulted in nothing. Their questioning email had been politely replied with a decline for further inquiry or explanation by the Administration department.

Since all four boys still questioned the government's ability to dictate the individual hubs regulations, they had settled on further research instead of questioning the Academy.

Miles was the best at this, but since schoolwork and the building of the Z-riders kept them busy, this left little time for personal research. Miles promised he would spend his two months' vacation studying the laws, but Zane felt that was an empty promise.

"Rafe." Zane asked suddenly when he confirmed Breanna and her friends were deep in their own discussion at the other end of the table. "What did your father do?"

"What?" Rafe asked as he turned his attention to Zane. "Oh, he was my grandfather's apprentice."

"What does your grandfather do?" Zane asked, he also wanted to ask why Waltson was interfering in Zane's own life, why he thought Rafe's grandfather was paying for his own education and also shielding him from the Primary.

"Grandpa Waltson, he's a Controller. Runs an electric station or something. That's why I'm here, I can't apprentice with him until I receive my fifth level." Rafe explained then took a rather large bite of his vitamin burger.

"Wal, I mean your grandfather, is he high up in the government?" Zane asked as a new fear crept into him. If Waltson was in the government, Zane might have more than Primary Kasher to worry about.

"Nah, grandpa doesn't like the government. Can't

stand all the ins and outs of protocol." Rafe said and was too distracted to see Zane's huge breath of relief.

"When do you head back home?" Breanna's question pulled Zane out of his thoughts and he turned to studied her for a moment.

"Right after the Graduation ceremony." Zane answered and saw her pout a little. The ceremony was held on different days for the various levels. Level one students had theirs first, two days after finals were taken. This meant he had two more days of worry before he knew if he had passed his classes or not. Parents were invited to the ceremony and then immediately afterwards, most went home to their families. Mia already had plans for a party, he just hoped there was cause for celebration.

"Will you message me?" She asked as Evan started to tease them.

"I will message you all." Zane said as he wrinkled his nose at Evan. "And make sure you guys are keeping up with the Z-rider's orders."

Zane's mind turned from Waltson and the mysteries that surrounded him to his business. Zane hoped that running the small business would keep him busy for the two months. He already had weekly trips planned between the Recycler's hub and Evan's hub.

Just because school was shut down for two months didn't mean the request for Z-riders would stop. They already have enough orders to keep them busy for most of the vacation time.

He told Mitch about Rafe's family that night. Mitch had been shocked and concerned to hear Zane's discoveries.

"You didn't tell him anything, did you?" Rafe's worried voice squeaked over the TWT.

"No!" Zane confirmed. "I didn't know what to say."

"Good. Until we know more, don't say anything else."

Mitch didn't have to tell Zane this, he already knew he didn't ever want to tell Rafe that he had witnessed his father's death. Even thinking about this had new nightmares appearing out of the darkness that night. He awoke covered in sweat and once again his head hurt.

Two days passed quickly; Zane spent some of the time building Z-riders or researching Adam Waltson. The research was difficult because he had to ensure Rafe and the others didn't discover his research.

Mostly he stayed awake and used his tablet to learn all about Adam. According to the Academy records, Adam had graduated level ten over fifty years ago. He had been nineteen when he graduated, meaning he had started at the Academy when he had only been nine. Zane thought this rather young, until he found an article stating that Adam's father had died a year before Adam had started school.

Adam's grandfather wasn't mentioned in either article, but the family lineage had some impressive jobs. Zane didn't know what the titles meant, only each held the word "Controller" within its lengthy name.

He scanned his government text and didn't see any of the job titles in there which confused him. He knew from Rafe that the job must be outside the government. He ran a search and found Adam's current job listed. 'Head Main Controller' had a description that confused Zane even further. 'The function of control which holds a high position to monitor and dictate all which falls under this position.'

He tried to find further details, but each was more confusing than the other. By the day of the ceremony, he had given up on his research of Adam Waltson.

Zane's mind turned to having to say goodbye to his new friends and business partners.

True he had trips planned to visit each of them. He also had scheduled weekly e-meetings where all four of them would communicate over their school tablets. But the thought of sleeping in his little bed in the small room shared with his grandmother made him feel a little sad.

For two months there wouldn't be any break outs of mad disc or zipping around together on Z-riders. He wouldn't hear Mile's soft snoring or Rafe and Evan joking with each other.

"Cheer up, before you know it, we'll be back here and having to study for our first level two tests." Evan's said as he gave Zane a punch in the arm on their way to the ceremony which was being held out on the main lawn and road in the center of the hub.

Chairs had been lined up in the center of the road which split the Academy from the medical facilities. A single isle split the chairs and a large dais with tables sat at the front of the assembly.

Head Dean Dickson wore a rather bright purple robe with a golden rope around his neck indicating his high level. His round face beamed as the students took their seats near the front.

Family members and friends sat near the back, some waived at their students proudly while others raised tablets and took photos or videos. Zane saw Rafe smile and wave and quickly looked over to see a pretty dark-haired woman sitting next to a man with bright red hair. When the woman waived, Zane guessed it was Rafe's mother. She had a small girl on her lap, who's hair was as bright red as the man next to her.

Scanning the seats, Zane hoped to catch a glimpse of Adam Waltson but didn't see any white-haired men near the trio. Turning back to face the front, he did catch a glimpse of Mia and gave her a quick wave.

The ceremony was long, Head Dean apparently used the yearly ritual to provide all those gathered with his wisdom. Zane thought the man just liked to hear his own voice as ten minutes into the speech, Zane found his mind wandering.

"Full of air this one." Evan said next to him and had Rafe silently chuckling.

"I heard this might take a while." Miles murmured.

Twenty-five minutes later, when it appeared the Dean had run out of breath, the assistant dean stood and started to spout out names of the first level students.

The procession line grew as students walked up to receive their final grades. This was the only time grades were given in person and not electronically. This allowed all students to attend the ceremony, whether they graduated that level or not.

If a student didn't' pass, they could remain at the Academy and retake the tests or choose to go home. Passing students would receive their certificate along with their grades. When they registered for the next level, then they would receive their next school years schedule two weeks before school started again.

Zane was so nervous as he approached the assistant

dean that he didn't realize Mathew Carlson stepped forward. It was the Financial Advisor who handed Zane his certificate envelope with a smile.

"I wanted to be the one to hand you yours and tell you how proud I am of you." Mathew said and patted Zane on the back.

Too shocked and scared, Zane smiled with a nod and after grabbing the envelope, followed Evan off the stage.

Students were to return to their seats afterwards, but Zane discovered that his friends stood clumped together as they ripped their envelopes opened.

"I got mine!" Rafe said and Zane thought he heard relief in his voice.

"Me too!" Miles said and they turned to see Evan waving his level one certificate around like a flag.

"How about you Z?" Rafe asked and smiled when he saw the golden certificate peek out of Zane's envelope. "Whoopee! We did it!"

EPILOGUE

Secrets

*A*dam Waltson wasn't as spry as he used to be. But when the need arose, he found his steps swift as he turned into the darkened corridor. He knew the way forward like the back of his hand, but the new human element which could now be found down in these tunnels might cause this passageway to hold the unknown.

Along now and keeping to the tunnel's corners, he quickened his pace when he neared the secret entrance. He hoped no one was down this far, and this was confirmed when the overhead lights remained dark, only his chest plate with its faint golden glow guided his way forward.

His hand hovered above the secret latch as he turned and looked about one last time. When he confirmed he was alone, he released the clasp. The needle prick of his finger was so familiar, he no longer felt its sting as it pierced his thumb. After the blood sample was taken, he placed his thumb to his mouth as he waited for the bolts to be released.

The swish of the well-oiled door brought a blast of stale air to his face. Quickly slipping inside, he closed the door behind him and took a deep breath of relief.

After his second calming breath, he turned and found the chart. Taking the clip off the peg, he turned to conduct the only job that had ever mattered here in the world he and his people were trapped in.

"Welcome Controller." The automated voice spoke as the lights of the platform glowed brightly. It took a second for his old eyes to focus on the secretive panels. Then the Controller moved over to the main panel and studied the colorful readings.

"Status." He finally stated and found his voice still a bit shaky from his jog to the hidden control room.

"Sections two and eight are showing signs of high levels of Oxygenation. Levels are within allowed parameters." The mechanical voice replied as the old man noted this on his chart. "Water levels have lowered by one tenth of a centimeter. Levels are within allowed parameters." Again, this was noted in the chart. "An anomaly occurred at 02:23 hours." With this statement the old man looked up quickly from his chart.

"An anomaly?" This time his voice didn't shake from exertion, but excitement. "Another one?"

"Affirmative." Came the computer's answer. "Two thousand kilometers from the last one."

"Confirm!" The demand came out with a big breath of air as old eyes studied the gages in front of him.

"Confirmed."

The blinking gages told the Controller information that several generations had been waited for. Excitement and dread filled the man as he hesitated with his hand over the tablet, unwilling to mark this new information down on his chart. Seconds and minutes ticked away while he fought his inner demons in silence amongst the blinking gages.

When his fear finally overtook him, he blinked away the tears as hope fell away much like the drops from his eyes.

"Delete." He finally said and turned away from the control panel to continue his job.

THE END OF LEVEL ONE.

BOOKS BY J.J. ANDERS

Genoa Chronicles

The Scholar

The Warrior

The Queen

The Fallen

The Hidden

The Gifted

The Exiled

The Betrayed

The Lost

Level Up

The Pipes

The Fixers

The Printers

ABOUT THE AUTHOR

JJ Anders powerful imagination and love of writing has spawned the thrilling new world and enchanting characters of Genoa. As a furious reader and devoted mother, her passion for storytelling reaches full bloom to bring her magical stories to life for the enjoyment of readers everywhere of all ages.

Her fantasy series will leave you begging for more.